F*cked-Up Shorts

Volume II

Sometimes it is nice to have something short to read. Something you can pick up, blitz through and enjoy without clogging up your otherwise busy day. Between you and I, Short Stories are actually my main reading material as I often struggle to get into longer works due to being busy with my own projects. The amount of great books I've started and never finished because I struggle to find the time. It really frustrates me and I always mean to go back to the book to finish them but - by the time I do… I've forgotten where I am at. A short story though… I can pick it up and read it within an hour or so, some take even less time, and still have the rest of the day to get my bits and pieces done. They suit my lifestyle perfectly and with people working longer hours in order to get the bills paid… I know it's not just my lifestyle short stories suit.

I also *love* writing them.

This Volume contains:

She

The Funeral

The Light

Glory-Hole

Hair of the Dog

Teeth

(Only available in Black Room Manuscripts 2) Eleven

SHE

1.

A different kind of make-up.

She was standing in her bathroom on the second floor of her mid-terraced home with no clear recollection as to how she even made it there.

Her hair - previously blond - was tangled and knotted in thick, red clumps thanks to the cuts on her face and head. Her nose was split across the bridge with fresh blood trickling out. One pupil was larger than the other with a nice shade of purple, yellow and black circling her right eye with a minor laceration above her left. She kept licking her top lip, keeping the fresh split wet in an effort to stop the sting from whenever it dried out and she found herself accidentally stretching her lip with changing facial expressions - mostly expressing pain and discomfort.

Even now, staring at the broken girl in the unkind mirror's reflection and safely in her own home - away from further harm, she didn't cry.

She glanced down at her dress. What was once a smart black dress which stopped just above the knees was now a ripped mess, wet with claret and unfit for anything other than the bin.

Running a glass - fetched from beside her bed in the next room - under the cold tap, she poured herself a drink of water. As she took a tentative sip, her top lip split again and she grimaced in discomfort. A second mouthful was bigger but went un-swallowed as she swirled it around in her mouth before spitting it out into the sink. What started as clear water was now tainted pink.

Setting the glass down next to the tap, she leaned closer to the mirror and carefully pulled back her bottom lip. One tooth missing from the bottom row with a second, next to the new bloody hole, cracked.

She leaned forward over the sink once more and spat out another mouthful of crimson before sitting down on the toilet seat, unable to stand any longer. Every muscle and every joint was screaming in pain - further proof, as if it were needed, that the wounds weren't just to her once pretty face.

She knew she should have gone to the hospital. The only reason she hadn't was because she had been through enough already. She didn't need to be poked and prodded and - more importantly - judged by the people who were meant to be helping her.

She didn't need the whispering voices talking about her, some potentially saying that she had brought it upon herself and got what she deserved. And then of course there was the police. She didn't want to have to make a statement telling them what had happened and deciding as to whether she wanted to press charges or not. And - when she told them she didn't want to be pressing charges - there'd be the disappointed, and frustrated, looks from the investigating officers.

Another asshole getting away with his crime because the victim was too scared to stand up and be counted. But that wasn't why she didn't want to say anything to the police. She would be happy for him to go to prison for what he had done to her but it wouldn't stop there.

There'd be a court-case as, no doubt, he would protest his innocence telling all who'd listen that she had got what she deserved. And she would have to stand up and give evidence with yet more judgemental looks from both the gallery and the jury stand.

She sighed.

Occupational hazard. These things happen from time to time. That's the nature of the business, not that it had happened to her before. Plenty of her friends, yes, but not her. Overzealous punters who got too enthusiastic or had a sudden change of heart and resorted to violence to make the point that they think the service provider is in the wrong for even accepting such a booking from a married man - even though, more than half of the time, the workers have no idea as to the background of the clients.

Speaking of business...

Her mobile phone was ringing in her over the shoulder bag by the bathroom door, where she'd dropped it. A constant buzzing from clients desperate to have their cock sucked. All these pathetic men in need and yet - would they be there for her now that she was in need? Of course they wouldn't. Unless, of course, they got something out of being there in return.

Desperate for something to take her mind from the pain she was feeling, she leaned over for the bag and dragged it towards her. When it was close enough, she reached in and pulled out her iPhone just as the caller rung off. The screen displayed sixteen missed calls. Busy - even by Saturday's standards.

Another buzz from her phone and another voice-mail message left just as the client had been instructed over on the site where she advertised; leave a message if I don't pick up and I will call you at the earliest opportunity.

These clients wouldn't be having their calls returned any time soon.

2.

Where She makes a living.

Two days in bed without a penny earned. Had it not been for the visible bruises and the pain she was in, she could have earned a fortune had she done two straight days in bed; something which she was mentally aware of and feeling additional pressure for as rent day was looming ever closer. Even before this had happened to her, despite being the popular new girl on the town, business was definitely slow.

With the electric meter already running on empty, and unable to get to the shops to put additional funds on the key, she couldn't help but lay there wondering whether she'd be able to do a deal with the landlord of the property. Thanks to the tenancy agreement she had signed, with the letting agency, she had the man's name and address. For a short time, lying there, she pondered whether she could get away with penning him a letter directly. A "Dear Sir" sort of affair in which she'd offer reduced, or even free, services in exchange for a reduction in the rent.

It was more of a fleeting thought which would occasionally creep back into the forefront of her mind. She wouldn't ever write such a letter, or - even if he was standing in front of her - ask him for such a deal. For all she knew, he was one of these straight-laced members of society who frowned upon what she did for a living. A man who'd sooner kick her out into the dirty gutters of the street than have some whore living under his roof and fucking all who came to visit.

Other thoughts drifted to the clients who'd phoned, leaving the messages, and wondering whether she could offer them a reduced rate if they popped over with the cash now on the understanding that the services would follow in a few weeks when she was feeling better. Would that be acceptable? Was it even worth trying? If it worked - at least it meant her rent would be paid for another month. And, next month, she'd be back on her feet and earning again.

She laughed to herself as she considered the saying "back on your feet and earning". It hardly applied to her, given that she made her money right where she was now, lying on her back. Although, to be fair, usually her legs were up in the air or over the shoulders of some punter as he slid inside of her with unrivalled enthusiasm.

Uncomfortable on her back now, she rolled onto her side. It was still painful but the pain was definitely starting to subside. That was one thing, though, and she still didn't dare look into the mirror to see the mess the man's heavy punches had made of her. She closed her eyes and tried to think of something else but it was too late. Every time she thought about how much her body ached, or what the man had done - her mind mentally played it back to her; each hit, each kick and the nasty names he had called her.

'Cunts like you deserve this!' being one such thing screamed in her ear before a heavy fist to the side of her head followed.

She remembered the first blow. It had come out of nowhere. On first impressions he seemed to be a normal John. If anything she thought he seemed a little nervous. Looking back though, thinking back to that first hit, maybe she had misread him and the nerves weren't for what he was *supposed* to do to her but what he actually *did* do to her? Maybe what he had done - the beating he had dished out - was the plan from the moment he initially called her for the booking? Some kind of sick need to administer pain to a stranger? But would someone do that? Would someone book a hooker only to give them a kicking in their own home? There was nothing stopping her from going to the authorities. He certainly didn't warn her from doing so. It couldn't have been planned. It must have been a spur of the moment thing - a sudden guilt for what he was about to do. After all - he didn't start raining down the blows until she was standing before him naked and fondling his flaccid penis.

His soft cock. Was that the reason?

With all of the names he had been calling her - was the real reason for the violence that he was embarrassed about his lack of erection? Usually - at that stage of the appointment - the client was standing to attention. Was the fact he couldn't get it up what made him see red?

She rolled onto her other side and tried to think about something else. It was pointless thinking of the various reasons as to why he could have suddenly flipped like that and, besides, not even that far down in her subconscious - she knew the real reason behind his hostility. She just didn't want to admit it to herself as it just made everything seem that much worse.

She closed her eyes. She didn't want to think about it. She didn't want to be the victim. She just wanted to get herself better and get back to making her living; earn enough money so that she could finally move on with her life and put all of this behind her with a fresh start.

3.

Back to Business.

It had been well over a week since her beating but the thoughts of the supposed-punter still plagued her as she welcomed a new client into her home for what was meant to be an hour's in-call appointment.

Most of the bruises had all but disappeared now. Those that hadn't were faint and easy to hide behind an additional layer of skin-toned foundation. Trickier to hide was the missing tooth from the bottom row, and the cracked one. Thankfully - so far at least - the new client hadn't noticed and, if he had, he wasn't bothered.

'You look stunning,' he said as he stepped over the threshold, turning back to get a proper glimpse of her as she closed the front door.

'Thank you,' she replied. 'Did you want to go through,' she gestured towards her living room, where she took all of her clients first. She believed it helped them to relax if the money side of the business - and initial conversations - were conducted away from the bedroom. It took away the pressure of knowing you were about to perform.

'Thank you.' The client kicked his shoes off and - leaving them in the hallway - walked into the living room whereupon he took a seat on the sofa. She joined him and purposefully sat close to him.

He fidgeted, clearly uneasy about the proceedings.

'Relax,' she purred, placing a hand on his leg.

The man laughed nervously, 'I'm sorry,' he explained. 'This is my first time.'

'It's fine,' she said. She actually preferred first-timers because they tended to be more thoughtful about what they were doing. Seasoned punters came into their appointments with the belief that only they mattered and that they could do, and say, exactly what they wanted. First-timers were also more gentle and more interested in the *girlfriend experience* as opposed to a quick fuck.

'Oh,' he suddenly remembered, 'this is for you…' He reached into his jacket pocket and withdrew a small amount of monetary notes. One hundred and fifty pounds to be exact, in a mixture of ten and twenty pound notes. He handed it over to his date.

'Thank you,' she said - standing up. 'I'll just get rid of this,' she continued before leaving the room for a moment. One important rule of being on the game; never leave the money around somewhere obvious where a punter might take it upon themselves to take it back again.

'You have a nice home,' the client said, even though he hadn't seen anything other than the outside, the hallway and now the living room. A lacklustre attempt at small talk whilst he attempted to calm himself down. If only she had known how long he had actually been sitting outside the house for. He had parked up an hour before the appointment because he knew that was approximately how long it would take for him to muster up the courage to ring her bell.

She walked back into the room and took a seat next to him again, immediately placing her hand on his leg flirtatiously. He shifted his weight a bit as he sat up, still clearly nervous.

'Do you know what would make you more at ease?' she asked playfully.

'What's that?'

'A massage.'

'A massage?'

She nodded. 'Definitely. I've been told I have magic hands.' She stood up and extended a hand towards her new client. 'Come upstairs. It will be nicer for you on the bed.' She knew that - if she got this right - he would come back time and time again.

Nervously, he took her hand and she helped to pull him up from the sofa.

* * * * *

As she led him up the stairs, he couldn't take his eyes from her perfect arse. The way the dress hugged it tightly, accentuating the curves beautifully before stopping just beneath them - allowing the client to get a teasing glimpse of the tops of her stockings. Suspenders attached to them. The suspenders, themselves, disappearing upwards where he longed to run his hands. He smiled to himself and felt the first of the nerves slowly start to dissipate. He'd made the right decision. There was nothing to be nervous about. He was going to have the time of his life.

At the top of the stairs, she led him through to her bedroom. It wasn't the room she used to sleep at night. The clients never saw that room. This was her *working* room. There was a large cupboard in the corner of the room where she kept her outfits, a queen-sized bed next to that with the finest silken sheets over them and - next to that - a small bedside cabinet. In the bottom drawer were the various toys she had purchased to please both herself and her clients, the middle drawer housed the poppers to ensure total relaxation - if required - and the top drawer was where she kept the protection. Tucked beneath the different packets of Durex, there were even some blue pills for the really nervous clients who needed some additional help to perform.

For the more risqué of the punters, there were some under-bed restraints tucked beneath the bed and tied to each of the posts. She turned to the client as he stepped into the room. His eyes were wide, like a deer caught in headlights. He wouldn't be needing the under-bed restraints.

Not for *this* appointment at least. Maybe during a future one…

4.

A Perfect Gentleman.

'Lie down on your front,' she informed the client after first telling him to remove his clothes. Just as she thought he would, he stripped down to his boxers and stopped there - too embarrassed to go fully nude. She didn't mind. When the time came, she knew the shorts would come off too. For now though, it was whatever made him feel more comfortable.

'Okay,' he said nervously. He crawled onto the bed and laid on his front with his head turned to the side; a view of the window and the trees dancing in the gentle breeze beyond the window pane helped to distract him from what was coming.

The mattress bounced as she climbed onto the bed too, straddling herself over his legs. Unlike the client, she remained fully clothed for now. Once in position, she leaned across to the bedside cabinet and opened the top drawer where the condoms were kept. Tucked away at the back of the drawer, next to latex friendly lubricants of various flavours and *sensations* was the baby-oil. With a flick of her thumb she popped the lid and tipped some in the palm of her spare hand. Setting the bottle down again, she rubbed both hands together to ensure they were both nice and slippery.

'Sorry if my hands are cold,' she teased as she pressed both palms against his shoulders. He flinched due to nerves and the touch of the working girl, not because her hands were chilly. Slowly - and somewhere between soft and firm - she started to massage his shoulders.

'That's nice,' he sighed.

'I told you,' she whispered, keeping her voice soft to help him relax, 'I have magic hands.' She continued, 'Don't get too comfortable, though, it's your turn next.'

By giving him a massage first, he'd be able to relax. By allowing him to then run his hands over her body - well that was when he'd get aroused. From there, the appointment would take it's natural course of action; the reason he had actually booked her for this hour.

'Look forward to it,' he said - already starting to feel relaxed in her company. He smiled as he recalled the reviews; each of them giving top marks for how she made the client feel at ease. They weren't wrong.

Seeing that he was beginning to relax and seizing the opportunity to discuss the appointment with him, she asked, 'Was there anything you were looking for in particular today?'

Every client was different with their wants. Some wanted oral and nothing more - both to receive and give. Some wanted none of that and just straight-up sex. Some wanted to be tied and teased, being brought to the point of orgasm only to be denied at the last possible minute before the enjoyable wind-up was started again and then there were those who only wanted a little mutual masturbation.

The question was - what sort of client was this?

With a little stutter, he answer, 'I... I was thinking we could have some oral and then... Maybe some anal?'

'Sounds good to me,' she purred as she ran her hand down the crack of his own arse, reaching underneath to gently stroke his testicles. He murmured in pleasure.

The nice thing about the website she advertised on was that it gave the opportunity to list what services she was and wasn't happy to provide. A section dedicated to her *likes* and another section, right next to the previous one, which stated her *dislikes*. This way it stopped for any awkward moments between client and working girl when the client showed up asking for something that wasn't provided - such as bareback sex, which topped her *dislike* list. It also cut down the amount of emails she received asking for services she didn't like although, unsurprisingly given the amount of chancers out there, the odd one still slipped through the net.

Anal was on her *likes* list on the understanding that it would be decided upon the day depending on the size of the client she was seeing.

Running her hands slowly up the insides of the client's thighs, she whispered, 'Roll over.'

The client rolled over, slightly embarrassed by the fact that he had an erection.

'Sorry,' he said, even though he knew it was A) Perfectly natural and B) Part of the reason he had come to visit her.

'Don't be silly. It's nice,' she smiled.

Reaching down, she gently stroked his shaft as he reached across to her - unsure of the protocol - and placed his hand on her leg. He closed his eyes and sunk down onto the soft mattress, enjoying the feeling of her hands running up and down his length.

Without asking, she leaned down and wrapped her lips around the head of his cock. He let out a long sigh. It had been a long time since he'd had a woman - especially as sexy as this one - perform oral on him. Opening his eyes he looked down at her and noticed she was looking straight back up at him, holding his gaze.

Letting his cock slowly slide from her mouth, she asked, 'Nice?'

He nodded. 'Thank you.'

She smiled. She'd seen a lot of clients over the two years she had been doing this but - to her knowledge - this was the first time anyone had said *thank you* during the appointment. Sure, they often parted ways with words of thanks but not during the session. Well, not during the *normal* sessions. During the appointments whereby she played the more dominant role, she often demanded thanks and - if the client refused to give it - she'd stop giving pleasure and administer punishment instead, usually in the form of a cane or paddle.

This man though - a real gentleman... Talk about polar opposites from the last client; the one who didn't give her thanks but gave her a beating instead. The punter she was with now, this was a real man. This was why she loved her job.

She went down again, enveloping his stiff manhood with her plump lips and - again - he let out a long sigh as she started sliding her mouth up, and down. Up, and down. Slow. Teasing. One hand on his shaft, stroking it in rhythm with the movement of her mouth. Her other hand clasping his testicles, gently squeezing. And his own hand - still on her leg, stroking the stocking-clad skin in time with her own movements.

As she increased the speed with which she worked the client, he suddenly sat up and placed a hand on her head - stopping her in the process.

'Wait!' he said, catching his breath. 'Wait!'

Releasing his cock from her mouth, she looked up - worried she had hurt him, 'What is it?' she asked.

'The dress... Can you... I mean... Would you mind...'

She laughed, still gently stroking him with her hand, 'What would you like?'

'Can you take the dress off?'

She smiled at him, 'Of course.'

5.

Damaged.

She climbed off the bed with a nervousness flowing through her system. Even though she knew she wouldn't have been able to stay fully-dressed for the whole appointment, she wasn't looking forward to the moment she had to disrobe. It wasn't because she was embarrassed about her body, or rather she wasn't *usually* embarrassed about her body - it was because some of the bruising on the skin, from the run in with the last *client*, was still yet to fade. True enough most had been covered up but there were some, deep dark blue, which were harder to cover and once you noticed those, the others - previously hidden - started to become more obvious.

The client sat up in the bed, with his back to the headboard, and watched his chosen lady whilst touching himself - maintaining the erection she'd created with so little effort. She was watching him too - not out of lust, as he viewed her, but to see his reaction when she stepped from the dress.

She reached behind herself and worked the back zip. She slid the dress off one shoulder. She slid the dress off her second shoulder and then - trying to appear confident - she wiggled her body until it slid down her frame. A helping hand passed her hips and she stepped out of it, kicking it to one side.

'Wow…'

She was standing there with matching underwear one. Black knickers, black bra, dark stockings and black suspenders.

'You look amazing,' he said.

'Thank you.'

She took a step closer to the bed, ready to climb back on to resume what she was previously doing when he noticed the first of the bruises.

'That looks like it was painful,' he said with a laugh. Had he known the reason behind the bruise, he would never have laughed. 'What did you do?' He noticed another bruise on the inside of her leg, just above the stocking top. 'And there...'

'I'm sorry... I tried to cover them up.' She felt embarrassed. A body she was once proud to flaunt now caused her embarrassment and made her feel awkward. In her head she was berating herself for coming back to work so soon. She should have left it until all bruises had faded. She was stupid to have come back so soon. All of these thoughts were picked up by the client.

'What happened?' he asked, shifting his body until he was sitting on the edge of the bed within touching distance of his hourly date. He noticed there were more previously unseen blemishes on her otherwise flawless skin.

'I understand if you'd like your money back,' she said, offering a get out clause. Had he taken the refund, it would have been her own fault for coming back to work so soon. She just hoped that - by offering the money back - he wouldn't leave a negative review which would put off future clients at a time when her body was bruise free once more.

The client was almost offended by her offer, 'I don't want my money back.' He changed the subject back to her, 'Are you okay? I mean - do they hurt?'

'Not anymore.'

it happened?'

_ned to him and made it far less serious than it had been but -
_ was the point? If she couldn't confess to a punter, who could she talk to about
it? And maybe talking about it would be a good thing - help her move on from
what had happened?

'A client had a change of heart,' she said.

'What?' He was shocked. 'A client did this? Why?'

She couldn't answer that. There were many reasons as to why he might have
done what he did but - without going back and asking him - she would never know
the real reason. She could only presume.

'Guilt?'

'So you think he booked you and then felt guilty about it so beat you?' He
couldn't believe what he was hearing. 'What kind of sick individual...' he stopped
in his tracks. There was no point ranting about the cruelness of human nature. She
didn't need to hear it. She had lived it. 'Is there going to be a court case or did he
plead guilty?'

She didn't say anything.

'You didn't tell anyone?'

Again, she stayed silent.

'I don't understand. Why would you want to save him from prison? He
deserves to be locked up for what he did to you...'

'It's not that I don't want him to suffer. It's... I don't want people looking at
me and judging me. I've had it all my life and... I don't want to be that person
anymore. I just want to forget that it happened and move on.' She paused a
moment, 'Is that bad?'

'Why would people judge you? Because of what you do? They're not worth worrying about. They judge others to try and make themselves feel better about their own body, or job or whatever. It's the ugly side of human nature and - by the sounds of it - you've seen the worst there is to offer. And - I'm sorry you suffered that.' He paused a moment and asked again, 'Are you okay now though? I mean - if you're not - we can reschedule. I don't want my money back and I'll happily pay again next time - it's not about the money. I just want you to feel okay.'

She smiled at him. He really was sweet. Why were there not more people like this in her life, she wondered. And then, just as quickly as she pondered the question, she answered it for herself too; because these people have special people in their lives. The only reason she was seeing him now was obviously because of some dark fantasy he had based upon the prospect of going with a woman such as herself. A thrill from paying for sex.

'Honestly - it's just a few bruises now. I'm fine. I promise.'

He leaned forward and pulled her closer to him. 'I just don't understand how anyone would want to hurt you.' He kissed the small bruise on the side of her stomach before kissing her again on the stomach. Another kiss on the bruise on her leg; a delicate peck through the silky stocking. 'And as for people judging you,' he said, 'ignore them. You're beautiful.'

For the first time ever with a client, she found herself blushing.

'More than that…' he paused a moment to kiss her stomach again. This time though, he pulled her black knickers down freeing her hardening cock in the process. He finished his sentence, 'You're perfect.'

She sighed as he put her cock in his mouth.

THE END

THE FUNERAL

1.

Before a funeral, there needs to be a death.

Hanging was out of the question for sure. It wasn't the fact that he was overweight that put him off from dancing at the end of a noose. If anything, people would often tell him he needed to put weight on. He was just worried that he'd step through the hatch in the loft, fall back into the main section of the house, and the rope would snap - as would his legs when he landed in a broken mess on the landing. No death but - instead - a lifetime confined to a wheelchair, unable to make a second attempt due to being paralysed. Yes, hanging was definitely out of the question.

The bathtub was out too and that was because of the silliest of reasons. Although he often favoured baths over showers, he didn't like being in there so long that his fingers pruned up - giving the impression he had the decrepit hands of a ninety-five year old. It was a silly reason because, once the toaster was dropped into the bath and he was instantly fried to death - he wouldn't see, or care about, his fingers. Even so, it was still enough to put him off from attempting anything water-related.

Blades slitting across his veins, whether they be in his neck or in his wrists, was out too as he didn't like the sight of blood. Again, giving the end goal he had in mind - it seemed a trivial thing to concern himself about but there you go. That was just the way his mind worked.

After a day thinking about the various ways to end his life, he opted for the oven. The oven would not be lit but the gas would be turned on. He would then stick his head in said oven and choke himself to death on the toxic fumes. A plan, he hoped, which would result in a feeling similar to going to sleep. A plan which, sadly for him, was over before it started when - instead of killing himself - he ended up cleaning the oven instead. By the time he was done, he was too knackered to bother taking his own life and - so - put it off until the morning. There was - after all - no immediate rush and it wasn't something he wished to hurry into. By putting it off, at least he knew he had a whole night of staring up at the ceiling and planning it through properly.

It was important to him that, whichever way he opted to go, he did it without any mistakes. Mistakes? He had made enough of those with his life. He had to get this right. His final act upon this Earth.

Please God, let me get it right. Don't give them another reason to laugh at me.

* * * * *

The room was illuminated by the glow of the laptop screen. Jason was sitting up in bed - propped up with a pillow - with the machine whirring away on his lap.

Despite being tired, he hadn't been able to sleep. Instead, his mind stuck on thoughts of suicide, he found himself Googling the most popular ways to kill yourself in the hope he would be able to find a technique that would be good for him to try.

Looking at the list, the ten most popular to be precise, there wasn't much he hadn't already thought of. For example, the tenth most popular was drowning but - again - it was the thought of his fingers going prune-like which put him off. And, if that wasn't enough, there was the danger of severe and permanent brain damage thanks to oxygen deprivation. Didn't sound much fun.

Then there was death by electric shock. Most people do it in the bath by dropping some electrical appliance in with them. Prune-like fingers and the risk of cocking it up meaning you're stuck with deep burns and severe neurological damage.

I don't think so, he sighed to himself.

If he wasn't interested in cutting himself. He didn't like blades, he certainly didn't like the thought of sticking them into his skin and - if he cocked it up - he wasn't interested in the scars either. A permanent reminder of how he had failed. And, worse than that, a sign to all those who saw the scars that he was a no-good failure too.

The suffocation was a non-starter thanks to a trigger in his brain telling him to clean the oven instead of ignoring the sticky mess and just taking lungfuls of the toxic gas in until he passed out and - soon after - died. Also… With the gas spilling into the room, what would happen if his mum came by the house to check up on him? She'd turn the light switch on and then - boom! He didn't want her death on his conscience too. She was the one person that loved him. He wouldn't want to harm her.

Jumping is the one reason he was put off from hanging himself. He was worried about getting it wrong and ending up in a wheelchair. The only way around that was if he headed into town and got to the roof of a skyscraper and leapt from there. The problem being - town was more than ten miles away and he didn't have the bus fare required to get there. Sure, he could have walked. He did think about it for a short time but - it was a long walk. And it was raining.

Do you want to do this or not?

With all the excuses going round in his head as to why certain methods weren't suitable, he couldn't help but wonder whether his heart was really in this whole killing himself business.

I do want to do it. I just don't want to get it wrong.

He slammed the laptop lid down, darkening the room immediately. He laid back on the bed, putting the PC to the side. It would have been easier if he lived in America. He was old enough to purchase himself a gun and - well - it's not hard to kill yourself with a bullet to the brain. It can't be hard. Cobain managed to do it whilst supposedly smacked out of his head on a large amount of heroin.

He sighed heavily.

There's no rush. The final payment demands only came in the post this morning. They gave him seven days to pay so - that meant - he had seven days before they sent the bailiffs round to collect on the unpaid debt.

Okay. Give yourself 7 days.

He rolled onto his side. Seven days was a good number. A week to put his stuff in order. A week to hide the dirty magazines, crusted socks beneath the bed and anything else that would cause his mother embarrassment.

He smiled to himself. It was the first smile in as long as he could remember. He just wasn't sure why he was smiling. Was he happy because he had decided not to kill himself immediately? Happy at the thought of having one more week to live? Maybe - in that week - he would be able to put things right and concentrate on living again as opposed to wasting time thinking about how to die. A week could be a long time.

He closed his eyes, still smiling.

One week.

A surprisingly happy dream - perhaps prompted by the thought of having a week left to live - was interrupted by the high-pitched ring of the house phone resting on the bedside table.

Jason sat bolt-upright with his heart pounding - a common reaction to the rare times the house phone interrupted his sleep. As his heart beat slowly returned to normal he glanced at the clock which rested next to the phone. Ten past three in the morning.

Who the Hell?

Jason leaned over to the phone and lifted it from its cradle before placing it next to his ear, 'Hello?' he asked cautiously. It wouldn't be the first time he had received a prank call in the middle of the night although he did think whoever was responsible for them had long since got bored and disappeared. That or - he hoped - they had died; a victim of Karma.

'Is that Mr. Payne?' a female voice asked.

'Speaking.'

'Mr. Jason Payne?' the stranger double-checked.

'Who is this, please?' Jason wasn't in the mood for fun and games. He was tired and - now - irritable from having been woken up from a good dream; something he hadn't had for what seemed like an eternity.

The irritated expression on his face dropped when the lady explained who she was and why she was calling. They'd received a 999 call. By the time... Jason switched off as his heart sunk and eyes welled-up. He was required to go down to the hospital to identify the body.

Mum?

2.

What once was filled with warmth.

Jason was led to the room where they'd kept his mother's body. She had phoned the paramedics, complaining of a tightness in her chest and a struggle for breath. By the time they arrived, she had suffered a massive coronary. They had tried, in vain, to bring her back but it was too late and she was pronounced dead on arrival. Now she had been left alone, covered by a thin sheet, in a cold room. Jason was standing at the door with his hands, and legs, visibly trembling.

The nurse smiled at him sympathetically. This was part of the job she hated. Even if the body on the other side of the door wasn't a relative and there had been a case of mistaken identity - which was rare - it still didn't give her any kind of satisfaction. Not only had they put this person through the worry of having to identify a loved-one but it also meant that the real relatives were out there still, somewhere, unaware of the death.

'Did you want me to come in with you?'

Jason shook his head.

'Take as long as you need,' the nurse told him. 'I'll be right here.'

Jason smiled at her. Part of him felt sorry for her. This couldn't be a nice job for her, especially in the middle of what was undoubtedly a long and stress-filled shift. How do you work in this sort of environment and then go home and carry on with your own life after all the grief and heartbreak you would have witnessed.

'Thank you,' he said.

He looked down at the door handle. It's such a simple act, to open a door, and yet here he was - frozen to the spot wondering whether he could go through with it. Of course he could, he told himself. He had to. No one else was going to do it. There was no one else. It was just him and his mum. And - now - it was just him.

Aware that the nurse was waiting and he was about to break down into floods of tears, he reached for the handle and pushed it down - opening the door. Before he had any more time to think about what he was really doing - or what he was about to do. He stepped into the room and closed the door behind him. The waiting nurse, despite being a professional, closed her eyes and waited - all the time wishing she were on another ward. The baby ward, for example. Sure, they had their really tough days too but… That was the ward which was also filled with the most joy.

* * * * *

Jason's mother would have hated this room. The white, clinical walls were depressing and it was cold. Her own home had bright, flowery wallpaper pasted to the walls and the place was always warm as though the heating stuck permanently on - even in the summer months. She would have definitely hated this room.

Other than the gurney in the centre of the room, the room was empty. On the gurney - covered by a thin, white sheet - was the body of what appeared to be a small person. Well, he might not have been able to see who was under the sheet but - the size was about right.

He hesitated a moment or two, swaying on his shaking legs, before nervously approaching the body. He had known that this day was going to come - all kids know that, if things play out the way they're supposed to, this day is coming. A cruel fact of life; everything dies. Knowing it is inevitable, though, doesn't make it any easier. You don't want your loved ones to ever die. No one really does but the truth of the matter was, she was no spring chicken. In her early-eighties and pretty frail. Her husband, Jason's dad, had died ten years previously after a long, messy battle with cancer - the fight that had first sent Jason on his downward spiral into depression and poverty with unnecessary days off looking after both parents when things got too much for his mother to cope with on her own. He paused a moment, closing his eyes from the reality of where he was, and pushed the thoughts from his mind. Now was not the time.

Opening his eyes he approached the side of the bed and hesitated again. The way his heart ached, he already knew that - beneath the sheet - his mother was dead. Some niggling, unpleasant feeling in the pit of his stomach told him so. Even so, he knew he had to pull the sheet back.

He reached out with his left hand still shaking and - carefully - pulled the sheet back exposing the pale face hidden beneath. He wasn't surprised to see that it was his mother. Her eyes, and mouth, were shut and her hair had been brushed back from her face. She looked as though she were sleeping peacefully which, at least, gave him some comfort. He just wished their last conversation had been nicer.

Visiting her, on a Sunday when he tended to pop over, she was in one of her moods - telling him that he needed to snap out of this depression he was in. She didn't understand depression. People of that generation rarely did. After all, Jason thought he was having a tough time but... She'd lived through so much before he was even born and not once did she appear down about it. The old saying, "what doesn't kill you, only makes you stronger" seems to have been right in this instance. For such a frail looking woman, she sure did have a lot of internal strength. Strength that Jason wished he had within him.

He hadn't been in the mood to hear his mum's lecture - when she started telling him to snap out of it - and he ended up making lame excuses before leaving her alone. Storming home, frustrated at her lack of compassion or understanding - he hadn't expected to never get the chance to talk to her again.

'I wish I told you I loved you more,' Jason whispered under his breath. A small part in him wishing she would say it back to him too - just one last time. He'd give anything to hear her voice say something kind. Something for him to remember her by as opposed to the last conversation they had shared.

A tear spilled from his eye and hit her cheek. He wiped it off with the back of his hand - gently so as not to move her - and then leaned down and gave her a final, loving kiss on the forehead. Her skin was cold. A chill which ruined the illusion of a peaceful sleep.

'I loved you, even when I said I didn't.' His mind haunted by years long gone - back when he was a young lad living at home and having one of the many bust-ups with his mother. The amount of times he had shouted at her how much he hated her, or that he wished she were dead. Years later – now that he had got the wish he had pretended to have he regretted all the times he had shouted it out loud. Angry words that were screamed to cause pain yet they were never meant.

She knows that. She always knew that.

Gently, he pulled the white sheet back over her head, covering her face. Wiping his moist eyes with the backs of his hands, he turned away from her and hurried from the room.

The nurse was standing in the corridor, still waiting for him. Without a word he nodded to her. She didn't need to ask the question. It was a positive I.D.

3.

Unwelcome distractions.

Before his mother passed away, Jason would wish for distracting thoughts which took his mind away from taking his own life. After all, suicidal thoughts can be distressing - even if you are desperate for your life to end. Planning his mother's funeral though wasn't the distraction he had hoped for. Especially as he didn't want a service in which he'd get to say his final goodbye as he didn't want to let her go. He wasn't ready to, especially with the heartache of the last conversation weighing heavily on his guilty mind.

He kept thinking, if only there was some way to turn back time to all the times he had been an asshole - or said something he now regretted to her - but this wasn't the movie or some cheap novel with a happy ending. This was real life and there was no going back. The only direction one could move was forward and - even then - that was only possible when you were able to forgive yourself for past wrongs. Something which, presently, Jason was unable to do.

He closed the local newspaper having read the obituary he'd had published in the back pages. Without knowing what to say exactly, he just mentioned her passing and when her service was going to be. He didn't know whether anyone would see the advert - was that the right word? - and, truth be told, he wouldn't have bothered had it not been for the local vicar suggesting it was a good idea. The cynical part of Jason - long since buried by depression and self-loathing - reared its ugly head, albeit briefly, to mentally question whether the church got a cut from the newspaper. For every obituary paid for by grieving families, the church got x amount donated to them.

To be fair, the vicar had been more than helpful with regards to helping Jason sort the funeral out. Unaware of his mother's wishes - as she never stipulated anything in particular and had no Last Will and Testament to speak of - the vicar had suggested to Jason that she might have liked to have been cremated like her husband. Jason would then be able to scatter her ashes in the same spot her husband had been scattered - a pretty flower garden nestled amongst the trees to the rear of the church. Jason had agreed and the vicar told him not to worry about any of the details with regards to organising it through the crematorium down the road for the church. All he had to do was pick a date for the service and the vicar would deal with the crematorium on his behalf.

'One less thing to worry about in this sad hour,' the kindly vicar had said. The church had remained in the same family for some time now. The vicar now, in his late forties, was the son of the man who'd overseen the wedding of Jason's mother and father so it came as no surprise that he wanted to be of as much help as he could. The church had known the family for over sixty years.

Although it wasn't a pleasant task, the funeral arrangements were fairly straight forward once the death was registered. Certainly straight forward enough not to have to purchase the services of a Funeral Director, again - helped by the fact the vicar was more than happy to help out where needed; even helping with the order of service.

'Did she have any poems that were special to her?' the vicar had asked after Jason first approached him to conduct the service.

'I don't know,' seemed to be Jason's standard response to him. He didn't know of any poems, he didn't know if there were any parts of the Bible she had liked, he didn't know if there was a particular song she would have wanted playing for when the mourners came and took their seats. A horrible feeling inside of him that - despite being her son - he really hadn't known his mother in these twilight years.

'Well if you want - I can get you some popular poems. Perhaps you would like to choose one we could use? The same with the hymns, if you don't know of any she particularly enjoyed, I could get you a list of ones that would be suitable. The bible reading, if you require one, I can organise for you. You can either read it yourself, or I can - whatever you are more comfortable with,' the vicar had suggested - an understanding smile on his face the whole time. There was no judgement being made here, he was just happy to help. Something Jason was particularly grateful for and - in the space of a couple of days - most things had been organised.

* * * * *

'How are you feeling?' the vicar asked, sitting opposite Jason in the grieving son's kitchen - a cup of tea and plate of biscuits in front of him.

'Like I'm on a rollercoaster and can't get off.' Jason was looking at the printed Order of Service. On the front was his mother's name along with a photo of her, standing proudly next to her son; a picture taken from her younger years. Inside was another smaller photo, more recent, and the words to a poem which Jason had chosen for her. Beneath the poem - a short summary of what was to be spoken about, including her life with her late husband and other key moments worth noting. On the page opposite there was one hymn; the words to *All Creatures Great and Small*. Again, it had been chosen by Jason. He didn't know if it was a song his mother particularly liked or not but he was well aware of the fact that it was popular and - if they had to sing it, which they would - most people knew the words and the way it was sung. After all, there was nothing worse than being presented with a song and being made to sing it without prior knowledge to the melody or words.

Closing the small booklet, there was another colour photo of his mother on the back. Beneath the picture was the date she was born and the date she passed away. Both dates Jason would never forget, not that he wanted to.

'It gets easier,' the vicar said. If anyone should know, it would be him with the amount of grieving families he had seen. 'And - of course - if you ever need to talk, you know where to find me.'

Jason didn't say anything. He set the Order of Service down on the table and took a biscuit. Taking a bite, he realised it had been the first thing he'd eaten in a few days now. Crunching it between his teeth, it almost felt alien to him and he nearly retched - an act that didn't go unnoticed by the vicar who smiled sympathetically before changing the conversation to save Jason from any potential embarrassment.

'So - tomorrow - the car will be getting there just before ten o'clock in the morning. I understand you want to help carry the coffin in?' Jason nodded. 'That's fine. Well… You'll take your mother in through the main doors and walk her to the far end of the aisle where she can be placed on the ready-prepared stand. Then, if you still want me to do the talking for you, you'll take your seat at the front. Don't worry about there being space - we'll clearly mark a seat out as being reserved for you.'

'Thank you.'

'You're happy with the Order of Service?'

Jason nodded.

'The whole service should take around twenty minutes. Then the congregation will be asked to stand as your mother is taken back out from the church and placed back into the hearse. You will then be driven to the crematorium where the other guests will be invited to follow. Here, a few more words will be said and people will have a chance to say goodbye to your mother before the curtain is closed.' He paused a moment wondering whether Jason had heard anything of what was said.

Jason was staring at the photo of his mum on the rear of the Order of Service, lost in thought - trying to remember when the picture was taken. She was sitting in what appeared to be a garden Jason didn't recognise. She had a glass of white wine in her hand and was smiling towards the camera, seemingly full of joy.

When was that picture taken?

'Do you have any questions?' the vicar asked, needing to be sure Jason understood how things were going to play out the following day. Jason visibly snapped back to reality and shook his head from side to side.

'I don't think so,' he said. 'It all seems fairly straight forward.'

The vicar smiled and took a sip of his tea. The milk was off.

4.

Remembering Mum.

Jason was staring at the closed casket. He knew his mother was inside yet - on
some levels - it didn't seem to be registering with him that she was really there. A
weird empty feeling flowing through him as he stared at the coffin, the droning
words of the vicar coming out as nothing but noise to him.

Jason knew what was happening was real yet on some level he refused to
believe it. He kept expecting her to come in and tell him to pull himself together, or
smarten himself up (if he ever wanted to meet a woman). Even though those
conversations annoyed him, well - they frustrated him, he still yearned for it to
happen one more time as he started remembering the good times they had shared;
such as the many beach trips during the summer holidays. His father had been too
busy with work to take them away, or do anything with his family, but his mother
would often make up for it by driving the two of them to the beach for ice-cream
and sandcastle building. Or there was the time she teased him after school, saying
he had to go to the dentist - scaring him - when, in actual fact, she was taking him
to the cinema to watch the latest Bill Murray film, *Scrooged.*

Other moments of happiness included doing a bakery class on a school open
day; a short lesson whereby he and his mother learned how to make biscuits. Or
the cartooning lesson they had enjoyed in the local *Hobbycraft* store - silly little
things that most parents wouldn't usually think of doing with their child. The less

pleasant experiences of being ill, yet having his mother to cry to; a woman who would clean up selflessly and make sure he had everything to be comfortable, even if she were tired after running around all day. A woman who'd ensure he had clean clothes on his back, a tidy room if he hadn't bothered tidying it himself, a shoulder to cry on when his first girlfriend dumped him, someone to go to the video store and hire out the films he was unable to due to being underage... Random memories all flooding into Jason's mind with no rhyme, reason or even chronological order.

But then - just as his memories always did - they turned darker in tone.

The woman he loved was now the monster berating him for this and that - some things being his fault and some things just because she was in a foul mood herself. Then it switched and she was on the receiving end of his spiteful remarks. He didn't love her, he wished that she was dead, he hated her, fuck off to name but a few examples in the montage playing through his mind... A montage that seemed to play over and over again with mental images somehow captured by his own mind; his mother with obvious hurt in her eyes, caused by the torrent of abuse aimed at her for whatever reason.

And the reasons themselves, for such vile language and comments? Usually pathetic and in no way worthy of such a vicious assault. Reasons which - as he sat there listening to the vicar drone on with his own account of the woman's life - made him feel terrible.

'Stop!' Jason shouted as he stood up.

With tears in his eyes, he approached the confused looking vicar who asked, 'Are you okay?' A fair question considering it was the first time he had been asked to stop a service that wasn't a wedding and - even then - he'd only been required to stop one of those a handful of times over the hundreds of services conducted.

'I need to say something,' Jason said - his voice quivering as he turned to the small congregation as the vicar stepped to the side. Jason stood there for a moment, unsure of what he was really doing. His mind was racing in a million different directions and he wasn't sure if any of them were good. 'I've not been the best of sons,' he said after a while. 'I've let my mum down more times than I can remember and - in recent years - when she needed me the most, I wasn't there for her.' He choked on the last sentence and forced himself to swallow back the tears as the guilt continued to weigh him down.

'She knows you were there,' the vicar said quietly from where he was now standing. A reassuring sentence that only Jason would have heard.

'That's not good enough,' Jason snapped. 'She should have seen me.' He turned back to the rest of the room and raised his voice so that people in the back row could hear him, 'I've called her some horrible things over the years. Things,' he continued, 'that I am not proud of and yet - through it all - she stood by me, supporting where she could.' He paused a moment, 'If it weren't for her I'm not sure I would be standing here before you admitting to all of this.' He looked sheepishly at the vicar as he knew suicide was considered a sin. The vicar didn't once judge him. He faced forward once more, 'I wish I could turn the clock back and have just one more day with her. Tell her I loved her and that I was sorry for all the grief I had given her over the years, often blaming her for my own poor attitude. I wish I could hold her once more and…' he went quiet as he struggled to contain his emotions. Tears started to roll down his cheeks.

'A parent loves their children unconditionally,' the vicar said to him. 'Your mother knows how you felt about her. She knows that - when you uttered hateful words - they weren't meant and were spoken out of haste and anger as opposed to from the heart… Your mother knows you loved her.'

Jason turned to him, 'I just wish I could tell her one last time. And,' he paused a moment, 'I wish I could hear it from her. I wish she was here to tell me that I have nothing to feel guilty about and that everything is going to be okay.' He wiped his eyes with the back of the hand and glanced back to the other faces seated before him. Older people, friends of his mother, looking at him with both pity and sympathy in their eyes. 'I'm sorry,' he said, 'I can't do this.' And - with that - he hurried down the aisle and out of the main doors.

The vicar stepped forward, 'Erm… If you'd like to stand and join with me in the singing of *All Creatures Great and Small*.'

With muttered voices, the congregation stood as the organ played the opening bars of the hymn. Moments later, they were all singing the words despite having their minds firmly on what they'd just seen.

Unlike ninety percent of the congregation, the vicar didn't need the word sheet in front of him - although he still held it there. He'd lost count the number of times he had sung this particular song. But, right now, his mind wasn't on that. He was watching the entrance, hoping that the doors were going to open and Jason was going to come back in. He couldn't hold the funeral up whilst someone went looking for him as they were on a timed schedule - especially down at the crematorium - but he hated the idea of Jason missing his mother's funeral. No one should miss the chance to say goodbye to a loved-one. However - from the start of the song to the end - the doors remained closed and that's where they remained until the end of the service.

* * * * *

Jason hadn't strayed far from the church and watched from the graveyard as the guests slowly began to filter out behind the coffin he was supposed to be helping to carry. Having given the talking responsibilities to the vicar, he had one job today - to help carry his mother - and he couldn't even do that. Instead, he noticed, a distant relative had stepped up and offered help.

Jason made a mental note to thank him later, at the wake which was being held at his own house for those who wanted to come over. As the coffin was loaded into the hearse, Jason slowly started making his way back over to the guests, ready to apologise for his behaviour - not that anyone thought badly of what he had done.

'Everyone handles grief differently,' the vicar told him as he approached. 'It's perfectly normal to do things you wouldn't usually do when you're suffering from grief. Especially given the pressure you put yourself under organising everything.'

'I didn't organise everything though,' he pointed out. 'I had you to help. And - thank you again for that.'

The vicar smiled, 'No thanks needed.' He reminded Jason, 'And if you ever need to talk… You know where I am.'

Jason smiled as his mind wondered whether the vicar would listen to his thoughts on suicide too and whether he'd be able to help him - not with the act of killing himself but rather the act of being able to talk openly about it in order to get the help he was desperate for. His mother's death made him realise, he didn't want to die. He just wanted help. That was why he had kept finding excuses not to go through with it. It was his subconscious telling him that he wasn't ready to give up the fight yet.

'Excuse me, sir, but we're ready to go.' One of the men from the Funeral Home interrupted Jason and the vicar. His mother was loaded in the rear of the hearse now with the back door closed and they were ready to head on down to the crematorium.

Jason nodded to the man that he understood and turned back to the vicar, 'Really - thank you for everything. You've done more than you could possibly imagine.'

The vicar smiled as Jason walked back to the main car, happy to have helped in whatever capacity he did. Despite the hiccup in the middle, it had been a good service with just this final stretch to go.

The last goodbye.

5.

Ash to Ash…

The trip to the crematorium was short. A fairly new establishment, only a couple of
years old and one Jason had never frequented before. Everything looked smart
from the brickwork building itself to the way the gardens were lined with rose
bushes. To the left of the crematorium itself was a covered driveway where the
hearse parked up; a place sheltered from any potential rain storm for when the rear
of the car was unloaded. Behind the crematorium, a paved area with rows and rows
of gold plaques, each naming a loved-one who'd been cremated here. In front of
these plaques, flowers.

Jason - and the other guests - were ushered into the building and urged to take
a seat. After what had happened at the church, proceedings were running a little
behind and the staff at the crematorium were fully conscious of the fact another
service was due to be taking place within an hour of this one. The last thing anyone
wanted, in these mournful times, was to find themselves stuck in a traffic queue as
people were getting rushed through as quickly as possible.

The room itself was large with cushioned seats all lined up; sixteen seats in a
row - with a gap running down the middle, and about ten rows deep. Jason was
sitting at the front, in the middle, feeling isolated even though he had people sitting
either side of him. His mother was on a stand at the front of the room. Next to the
coffin was a large framed picture of her standing on a wooden A-Frame. Either side

of the frame, there were pretty white flowers.

When everyone had their seat, the vicar walked to the front of the room and stood to the side of the casket - opposite the flowers and picture. His hands were crossed in front of him as he made his final speech about Jason's mother and how she was now in the hands of the Lord Almighty.

Jason closed his mind to both the words spoken by the vicar and the guilty thoughts which still plagued him. He just needed to get through these next five minutes or so, without any embarrassing incidents, and then he was done.

The vicar continued, 'We have been remembering with love and gratitude a life that has ended. Let us return to our own homes and to our work, enriched and inspired by these memories.' There was a slight pause before he finished, 'Would you please stand for the committal. To everything there is a season and a time to every purpose on earth, a time to be born and a time to die. Here in this last act, in sorrow but without fear, in love and appreciation, we commit Rose to her natural end.' He turned to look at the coffin and no sooner had he done so, *We'll Meet Again* started playing on a stereo - operated from the corner of the room by one of the crematorium's staff. After a few bars, a curtain started to silently surround the casket.

Jason wiped a tear from his eye. This was really happening. She was gone and wasn't coming back. He was alone. Even in a room full of supposed friends and relatives from his mother's dwindling side, he was alone. He looked up, worried about what the future held, and caught the eye of the vicar who was still smiling sympathetically at him. Jason smiled back out of politeness and remembered the words spoken by the vicar on two occasions now; the offer of being there as an ear to listen if Jason ever needed to talk.

Jason *did* need to talk.

With the music still playing, another staff member opened the side doors to the room which led out onto the patio area where the gold plaques and flowers were. One by one, the mourners slowly started to filter out to pay their respects at the area reserved for Rose's floral tributes; beautiful bunches of flowers which had been brought over by the mourners themselves and laid upon the paved floor next to yet another picture of the elderly lady. Jason didn't follow them. Instead he approached the vicar who was standing to the side of the door, waiting for the room to clear.

'Thank you again for today and sorry about earlier,' Jason said.

'You have nothing to apologise for. Like I said, we all deal with grief differently and - to be honest - it was probably better that you said what was on your mind just to get it off your chest.'

Jason changed the topic of conversation, 'You said that if I ever needed to talk, you were there… Did you mean that?'

The vicar frowned, taken aback by the desperation in Jason's voice, 'Yes. Of course I did. My doors are always open to you.'

'I was wondering if you had time for a little chat. You see, I've been having these thoughts recently and I do not know who to turn to.'

'What sort of thoughts?'

'I've wanted to hurt myself. As in - I wanted to die.'

There was immediate sympathy on the vicar's face. Through his years of service at the church, people had often come to him with their problems and never once had he turned anyone away. And this particular problem was something he'd heard a lot - surprisingly. He might not have been trained to give proper advice but he was a good sounding board and - fully prepared for such conversations - he knew people who *could* help. Professionally trained individuals who'd be able to help the distressed with both therapy and medication.

Jason continued, 'It's not since my mother died either - before you ask. Before then. It has been for a while now.' Jason wiped another tear from his eye before it spilled down his cheek. 'Sometimes,' he continued - almost embarrassed by how pathetic he thought he sounded, 'I cry myself to sleep as I play through - in my head - the various ways I'd take my own life.'

The vicar didn't want to turn him away but he was aware time was running out before the next service was due to arrive at the crematorium. 'Listen,' he said, 'I can't talk now but… Are you able to come to the church tomorrow morning for a chat? I have the morning free so we can talk through everything that is worrying you.'

Jason nodded, 'I can do that.'

'And perhaps we can think of a way forward whereby you don't want to hurt yourself?'

'I'd like that.'

'Shall we say about nine o'clock? I mean, of course, it's not a problem if you wish to come down earlier…'

'Nine o'clock is fine.'

'Good.'

'Listen - again - thank you for everything you've done. I really do appreciate it.'

'Honestly, it's not a problem.'

'Well, okay then, I'll see you tomorrow.' Jason smiled at him before stepping out into the fresh air. For the first time in as long as he could remember he felt the heat of the sun beat down upon his face and warm his blood, he smelt the freshly cut grass and remembered summer days long since gone - playing in his garden with his mum and dad watching from the patio table and chairs. He wasn't stupid enough to think that everything was fixed and his life would be perfect. He knew he was a troubled-man. He had debt. He didn't have a partner. His parents were dead and he felt as though he didn't have any real friends - at least, no real friends that he could talk to but… Since talking to his vicar he finally felt a small glimmer of hope. And - to think - all that was needed was for someone to offer him their ear.

'I'll see you tomorrow,' the vicar called out after him as he closed the doors to the hall - shutting himself inside.

Jason looked at the floral tributes laid out for his mother. She would have liked this. Flowers of varied colours all bunched together beautifully. Actually, Jason thought, she wouldn't have liked this, she would have *loved* it. Just as she would have loved the idea of Jason starting to get his life back on track.

He looked up into the cloudless sky and smiled as the sun's rays continued beating down upon his face, 'I'll do this for you, mum,' he said to himself quietly. 'I'll make you proud.'

There was a long way to go and a lot of problems and issues to fix but at least he felt as though he stood a fighting chance now. He laughed to himself again, *and all it took was for someone to show they cared and were there to hear him.*

The man, he thought, is a Saint.

* * * * *

Down in the basement of the crematorium was where the bodies were burned. A large chimney system filtered the smoke out as the remains of the bodies were reduced to ashes before being put in urns and given back to the grieving families at a later date. It was a room closed off to members of the public due to various reasons with one of the main ones being down to health and safety.

At the top of the stairs, the door labeled "staff only" opened and the vicar appeared. He stepped onto the short landing space and shut the door behind him before coming down the stairs, removing his white collar in the process and running his hand over the back of his neck as though the collar had been irritating his skin.

'Where's Rose?' he asked of Jason's mother as he reached the bottom of the stairs.

The owner of the crematorium was standing by the oven, looking at his watch, 'She's in the oven,' he said with a simple nod of his head. 'How did you want it?'

The vicar joined a couple of the other staff members who were sitting at a table in the centre of the room. He lifted a napkin from the table-top and tucked it into the front of his black shirt before picking up his knife and fork. 'Medium-rare for me,' he said.

This was the part of the service he loved the most.

'She smells Godly,' he said, licking his lips.

'Indeed she does,' the second man replied. 'Leg or breast?' He opened the oven door and - reaching in with special gloves - he removed the metal tray containing Rose's cooked body. Her hair was singed off and her skin had darkened - crisping in the process. Beneath the top layer, though, the meat was cooked to perfection. And the smell? Heavenly.

'Breast for me.'

THE END

The Light

1.

Suzanne didn't want to go to the cinema with her husband and kids. It had been a long day working in the same coffee shop she had been stuck in for the last fifteen years and she just wanted to go home and relax with her Kindle device. Perhaps a long soak in a hot bath? Maybe add a glass of wine, or two? End the quiet evening with an early night. Bliss. And anyway, even if she weren't so damn tired, she didn't fancy the film. Truth be told, neither did her husband Dwayne. He'd have rather taken Shyila and Kayla to their film and then gone into some over the top action film, or a horror film. Anything other than a crappy film based on a child's annoying television program. Plus side, he said to Suzanne, it would at least be short. Filmmakers know better than to drag a kids' film out for longer than entirely necessary - given the average child's attention span.

Suzanne leaned into her third child's bedroom. Three year old Isaac was fast asleep in bed. The perks of it getting dark so early at this time of the year was that it was easy to convince him it was bedtime. Although - that being said - it did mean he needed his night-light to be switched on before it was even dark on the off chance he woke up during the dead of night. Still - getting him to go to bed early, believing it was much later than it was… That was definitely a plus side. A sneaky trick and one that she couldn't get away with for much longer but - whilst it worked - why shouldn't she use it as much as she could? She smiled at the sight of him sleeping peacefully. Given she planned a relaxing evening for herself, she had half-expected him to act up. Especially when the others let slip that they were going to get some pizza before watching a film at the cinema and he wasn't! It's not as though he wouldn't have enjoyed the film, it was just that it started too late for him. It would be half nine by the time they get home and that was bordering on too late even for an eight and ten year old, let alone a three year old. He would have been miserable watching the film tired and he would have been miserable all tomorrow. As it was, he went to bed excited having been told he could choose what they did tomorrow. Within reason... And as for the pizza - Suzanne had bought Isaac a small one which she cooked in the oven for him. With him being so young, it was easy enough to trick him by saying it was from the same pizza shop and that she'd gone and collected it for him. Probably the fastest he had ever eaten his dinner.

Not that Isaac was a light sleeper, Suzanne quietly closed the door to his room. She walked down the hallway of her three bedroom home, towards the bathroom. The tub was three quarters full of hot water already. The bubbles were close to spilling over the edge, not that she cared. There was a towel on the floor to stop the tiles from becoming wet and slippery. Suzanne turned the taps off with a quick twist of her wrist and tested the water by dipping a finger in. Not too hot.

Not too cold. Perfect. She smiled to herself. All she needed now was the bottle of white she had purchased specially for this evening.

2.

The Kindle's screen illuminated the near-dark room. When Suzanne had first climbed into the bath, she hadn't bothered with the light. The sun was still shining beyond the window and there was no need for it. Yet just over an hour later, the sun was gone. The blue skies replaced with black. It was such a miserable time of the year but it wasn't just the light outside which had changed. The bath water had gone cold now too and the full bottle of wine was now only half-full.

Suzanne set the Kindle to one side having finished the latest chapter. A good place to pause so that she could get out, dry and warm herself under the thick duvet covering her comfortable, welcoming bed. She let out a heavy sigh. Whilst the thought of the warm bed was pleasant enough, she hated having to get out of a bath. There was always those few minutes where you found yourself freezing, frantically trying to dry yourself with the towel to get warm. She thought it was cool in the bath but she *knew* it would be colder out of it.

She glanced over to the radiator across the room. Before getting into the tub, she had carefully draped the biggest, fluffiest towel over it - warming it up so that it was ready to just wrap around herself. Just a couple of cold feet between her and warmth.

Okay, this is it.

Before she had a chance to change her mind, she pulled herself up and out of the bath. The cold air hit immediately and goosebumps rose up on her skin. Without pausing, she reached out for the towel and yanked it off the radiator before wrapping it around her naked, dripping body. The warmth from the heating offering comfort within seconds. Turning back to the tub, she reached down into the depths of the water and pulled the plug from the plug-hole. The water immediately started to swirl down with a heavy gurgle from the drains.

The wine glass and bottle caught her eye. She knew she should have taken it downstairs now but - truth be told - she couldn't be bothered. She just wanted to climb into her bed and get stuck into the next chapter of her book, some horror story about an evil presence in the woods. She was enjoying it and needed to know how it ended and yet she *knew* it would give her nightmares. Not necessarily because of the content itself but because she was picturing the woods out the back of her house when she was reading it. Considering the author didn't give any specific details of where the book was set in the world, it had morphed into her own woods before the end of chapter two as a result. And - if anything - that made it scarier. Still - she liked horror.

With the bath slowly emptying, all that remained was to brush her teeth, comb her dark shoulder length hair and then climb into bed.

Bed. Can't wait.

3.

'Rock and roll,' Suzanne laughed to herself as she slid between mattress and duvet, Kindle in hand. Friday night, not even nine o'clock yet and here she was in bed. Thirty six years old, going on a hundred. 'Who cares?' It wasn't as though anyone knew and even if they did - so what? So long as she was happy that was all that mattered and - right now - she was happy. She propped herself up against a pillow and tucked the duvet up around her.

Paradise.

The Kindle screen lit up at the press of a button and the next chapter appeared on screen, ready for reading. Suzanne took a swig of water from the glass resting on the bedside cabinet and then turned her attention to the screen. As she started reading she tried to mentally prepare herself for what was coming next. She knew this author. She had read most of his books and she knew he was an asshole when it came to the endings. It didn't matter how slow a story might have appeared, there'd always be a twist there that would slap her in the face and haunt her for days - sometimes longer - afterwards. Given this book appeared to be pretty mild for him so far, a happy story about a family going on a camping trip before the eldest child goes off to join the forces, she knew it was going to kick off. This author… He didn't do happy endings. Even in the non-horror books he penned, he tended to avoid the "and they all lived happily ever after" - even going as far as to be interviewed saying that endings like that are an insult to the reader.

Life isn't like that, he once wrote, *and sometimes the bad guys win.*

The author's statement once prompted Dwayne to ask, 'Why do you read these stories when you know he's just going to kill all the characters anyway?' It was a fair question but Dwayne missed the point of the author's books. Yes, the author was going to rain hell-fire down on the characters but - the reason she read the books - wasn't to see if they were going to live or die. It was because she wanted to see the twist. She wanted to know *how* he was going to mess with the characters.

'It's all a bit sick!' Dwayne said when Suzanne explained the end of one book to him, a cheerful little story about a man keeping a woman hostage in his house in the hope that she would fall in love with him. The author didn't do love. But the author did do a great *penis-biting* scene with copious amounts of blood gushing everywhere.

Suzanne chuckled to herself. Here it comes now. A character has just revealed his true nature and the husband of the family has found himself being buried alive. Here we go, this is where the trademark *sickness* comes in and Suzanne knew the remaining pages were going to gallop by at an alarming speed.

This is why she reads this author. This is what she wants. Escapism from an otherwise mundane life as she found herself hating work and wanting more. On the Kindle page, the husband screamed as the dirt continued to get shovelled down on to him. Suzanne rooted for the villain of the piece. The husband character was a dick anyway…

A heavy knock on the door startled Suzanne. A single thud against the wooden frame of the front door. A second went by and then another heavy thud. 8:45pm. Who, or what, on earth could it have been?

Not wanting Isaac to be disturbed, she climbed from her bed and quickly put a dressing gown on as a third heavy thud echoed through the house. Whoever it was, they were going to get a mouthful, that was a given.

4.

There was a fourth heavy thud on the door before Suzanne managed to get to it in time. Thankfully Isaac hadn't stirred from his bedroom, suggesting he was still asleep. But not for much longer if this idiot kept hitting the door.

Suzanne pulled the door, 'Please stop hitting my…' She stopped suddenly. A man in a smart, black suit was standing in front of her. Piercing blue eyes stared directly into her own. She finished her sentence, 'Please stop hitting my door, my boy is sleeping.'

'I'm sorry.' The man spoke with a slurred speech. His eyes locked to Suzanne's and yet he appeared to be looking straight through her at the same time. An uncomfortable silence fell between them.

Suzanne asked, 'Well? Can I help you?'

'I'm sorry?'

'Is there a reason you were knocking on my door?'

The man looked at her confused. He blinked a couple of times.

'What did you want?' Suzanne asked, growing ever more frustrated.

'The light was on.'

'What?'

'The light was on.' The man looked up to the light hanging from the ceiling above Suzanne's head. Suzanne followed his gaze before looking back to the stranger with a puzzled frown on her face.

'Please don't knock again,' she told him. She closed the door on him and took a step back without taking her eyes from it. Despite the man's smart appearance, she felt uneasy. The way he spoke was strange, the way he seemed to look through her and the fact he seemed to knock on her door for no reason. Hell, even his knock - a heavy, single thump against the door seemed unusual. Who knocks like that? She turned away from the door and started towards the stairs once more - a calling from her bed, and book, after a quick check on Isaac.

THUMP

Suzanne froze on the spot. Her heart had jumped, skipping a beat. Slowly she turned back to the front door and waited to see if it was a one off. Perhaps he hit the door out of frustration before storming off to annoy someone else?

'Hello?' she called out. Her heart in the back of her throat. No answer.

THUMP

'What do you want?'

No answer.

THUMP

'Please leave!' Suzanne called through the door.

THUMP

'I'm calling the police!' she warned.

THUMP

'What do you want?!' she screamed.

'The light is on,' the man said from the other side of the door.

Suzanne leaned to the far wall, next to the door and flicked the light switch, killing the light in the process. She stood there a moment - in the darkness. Quietly she crept towards the door and leaned close to it, straining to hear what (or who) was on the other side of it. There was silence and - then - the sound of shuffling. Someone, out there, moving from one foot to the other and then begrudgingly walking away from the door.

Suzanne breathed a sigh of relief. Whoever it was, he was gone.

She started to laugh to herself at just how freaked out she had gotten over it. Resisting the urge to open the door, to check he'd really gone, she walked through to the kitchen. She flicked the light on and took the kettle from the worktop. She was wide awake now with adrenaline surging through her body. Nothing a hot cup of tea wouldn't help calm. After filling the kettle with water, she set it back on the side and turned it on before resting back on the kitchen unit. She still felt uncomfortable. The man's voice, the look, the way he had thumped the door - all of it played on her mind. On the plus side, she thought, her own husband would be home soon enough. Another forty minutes maximum; that would take them to the time he estimated to return. Forty minutes.

Suzanne reached into the top cupboard and pulled out a mug.

THUMP

She spun to the back door where the sound had come from, as the mug crashed to the floor - shattering into pieces.

5.

The man was standing at the back door. At least, she presumed it was the man. The frosted window made it impossible to see anything other than a silhouette of the visitor. The way he knocked though and the general shape but... Suzanne *knew* it was the same person. Even though, she found herself calling through the door, 'Who is it?'

THUMP

'What do you want?!' She found herself getting more frantic.

'The light is on.'

'Of course it's on. It's my fucking house and it's dark outside!'

THUMP

She realised now that the man wasn't knocking with his hands but was - instead - banging the doors with his forehead.

THUMP

'I'm calling the police!' Suzanne hurried through to the hallway where the phone was resting on a small table. She lifted the receiver and pressed it against her ear, readying herself to dial 999. She paused. There was no dial-tone, only the sound of fluttering - like a million butterfly wings. A broken line. Suzanne pressed down on the base-unit's receiver before lifting off again, hoping to have got the line working once more. Still nothing but the strange sound. She slammed the receiver down again and paused a moment. Maybe that was all that was needed? Maybe the man - whoever he was - had been frightened off?

Slowly and quietly, Suzanne crept back through to the kitchen.

THUMP

Suzanne jumped and immediately turned the kitchen light off, plunging her into near darkness. The only illumination from the room coming from the still-boiling kettle. The figure beyond the frosted window hesitated a moment and then stepped to the side - out of Suzanne's sight. Just because the figure was gone though, Suzanne didn't move. She didn't dare for fear of him coming back. In her mind she kept telling herself that her husband would be home soon... He'll be home and then everything would be okay. If the person is still loitering around out there, he'll get rid of them. And, even if they've left, he will still make Suzanne feel safer.

The kettle clicked, signifying that it was done boiling, and Suzanne jumped again. Damned stranger had put her on edge. She moved through the darkness and pulled the kitchen blind down over both the door and the window. Only when both blinds were down did she dare turn the light on again. She paused a moment, half-expecting to hear that heavy thump against the door once more. She waited. Her heart was racing - a heavy, uncomfortable thump banging on the ribcage almost as hard as the man banged on her doorways. Waiting. Expecting. No sound from outside, though. At least - no sound of anyone trying to get in. Only a *dink-dink-dink* noise from within the room, coming from above her. Suzanne looked up. A large moth had somehow got into the room and was repeatedly flying into the light hanging from the ceiling.

'Great! That's all I need,' Suzanne muttered to herself. There weren't many things she was afraid of in life but - along with dentists - moths was definitely one of her phobias with their tatty looking wings and furry faces. A shiver ran down her spine and she turned the light out again. She wasn't that desperate for a cup of tea anyway. It could wait for Dwayne to get home… Which wouldn't be much longer.

Please hurry up, Dwayne.

THUMP

Suzanne looked up to the ceiling. The noise came from upstairs. The noise came from…

'No!' Suzanne hurried out of the room and up the stairs towards Isaac's room.

6.

Suzanne screamed when she opened the door to Isaac's room. Isaac was out of bed, standing next to the open window. The man - still dressed in his immaculate suit - was standing next to him with his hand on the boy's shoulder.

'The light was on…' The man spoke calmly as though his actions were perfectly normal and his being in the room entirely justified.

'Get away from my boy…'

Isaac looked terrified.

'He's a good boy.' The stranger stroked Isaac's cheek softly with the back of his hand. Suzanne noticed there were some moths on his bare flesh. Another shiver ran down her spine and she wanted to scream stopping herself only because she didn't want to scare her son more than he was already. The man nodded towards the dimly lit night-light and he repeated himself again, 'The light was on.'

'Please - get away from my boy,' Suzanne spoke calmer this time hoping it would be enough to get the man to release his grip from Isaac's shoulder. 'Please…'

'The light was on.'

'I know. I know it was. Isaac likes the light. He doesn't like it when it is dark… Please… Let my boy go…' Suzanne was fighting back the tears, fearful for what this man was planning for her and her boy. *Come on, Dwayne, please come home now.* 'Please tell me - what do you want? Why are you doing this?'

'The light was on.'

'I know the *fucking* light was…' Isaac started to cry stopping Suzanne mid-sentence. Getting angry at this man - whoever he was - wouldn't help. It would only make him angry and Isaac more afraid. 'Please - just get away from my boy.'

'We like your boy.'

Suzanne noticed some moths crawling on the man's skin around his shirt collar. She wanted to scream and to keep doing so until someone in one of the nearby houses alerted the authorities or came round, ready to kick the door in. But - of course - she kept it all contained within, bubbling beneath the surface for the benefit of her son.

'I love my boy.'

'Bright.'

'Yes, he is.'

'Could take many of us to the light.'

A moth crawled from the man's hand onto her son's pale skin. Isaac didn't even seem to flinch even though the thought of a moth landing on Suzanne's own skin caused her heartbeat to rise to an uncomfortable level and sweat to start beading on her forehead.

'I don't know what you mean,' Suzanne said. 'Please just let go of my boy. If you like the light… Come downstairs. You can sit in the living room with me. There are two lights in there and they get really bright. Much brighter than this. Please…' The man stepped forward slightly. Suzanne noticed that his eyes didn't seem quite as bright as when she had first seen him standing in the doorway. She guessed it was because there was no overhead light shining into them. It wasn't just that that she noticed though. His skin seemed to be paler now. a little more wrinkly too as though between downstairs and upstairs he had somehow aged. Suzanne said nothing other than to carry on with trying to coax him away from her boy. 'It's much brighter downstairs. You'll like it.'

'The light will fade as it always did. We need a brighter light to see us through.' The man looked down to Isaac. 'The boy is a bright light.'

'No. He isn't.' Suzanne called Isaac, 'Come to mummy, Isaac… It's okay. Come here.'

The man's gripped tightened on the boy's shoulder. Another moth came from beneath the shirt and crawled over his hand and onto Isaac's bed clothes. Suzanne watched in horror as the moth worked its way down Isaac's top. Isaac continued to stand there crying.

'Get away from my boy.' Suzanne warned the man again.

'He will lead us to bright lights for longer.'

'He won't lead you anywhere. He is my boy. He isn't going anywhere.'

Another moth crawled from man to boy. It didn't get unnoticed.

Suzanne suddenly shouted again, 'Get away from my boy!' This time, with her words, she rushed forward with the simple plan of snatching her child away. The man screamed at her with both his eyes and mouth wide open, a scream which stopped Suzanne in her tracks. She too screamed when - suddenly - large moths started flying from the man's mouth, right towards her. Fluttering around her head, around her body, lots of various-sized wings. The first moth entered her mouth, followed by the second. She closed her mouth after gagging them out. Isaac was screaming now too - a scream which got louder when the man standing between his mother and himself, suddenly exploded into a million or so moths, filling the room, dancing through the air, surrounding both panicked mother and terrified son. So many moths in the air that the dim-light, shining from where it was plugged into the mains, went black - seemingly off.

7.

The front door opened and Dwayne stepped into the hallway. He flicked the light on as Shyila and Kayla entered the house behind him, pushing past.

'Straight upstairs and get ready for bed, you two.' Dwayne told them as he closed the door behind him, locking it for the night. He turned round curious as to why he couldn't hear the pitter patter of little feet running up the stairs towards their bedrooms. They were standing at the foot of the stairs. Both of them were looking up at Suzanne who was standing there with her hand resting casually on Isaac's shoulder. Both of them looked different somehow. Their eyes bright and staring down at the rest of the family.

'Didn't see you there,' Dwayne said. 'You alright?' His question was directed at Suzanne. He took his coat off and put it over the bannister. 'Tell you what,' he continued without waiting for an answer, 'you really didn't miss anything. I think I fell asleep within ten minutes of that film starting!'

'He snored!' Kayla said.

Suzanne didn't say anything. She just stared down at them.

'You okay?' Dwayne asked Suzanne outright.

'That light is bright,' Suzanne said.

Dwayne frowned. Something was off. Her voice was different.

'You okay?' he asked again, hoping for an answer.

Both Isaac and Suzanne opened their mouths wide.

The light flickered for the last time.

THE END

Glory-Hole

I

Karen picked the framed photo up from the living room mantle-piece and looked at the happy couple captured within. It wasn't her, or her husband. Sorry - ex-husband. Or rather, soon-to-be ex-husband. It wasn't even her living room. With a slight pang of jealousy towards her friend and boyfriend, she set the picture back where she found it and stared at herself in the mirror hanging on the wall in front of her. A large ornate mirror hanging above the mantle-piece, reflecting most of the living room. She sighed heavily where she saw herself. She looked old. Bags under her eyes aged her prematurely. New lines around the eyes too thanks to a lack of fluids. Twenty-nine years old going on sixty-nine. She looked like shit.

From the coffee table behind her, her mobile started to vibrate. Despite knowing it wouldn't be him, she couldn't help but get her hopes up. She hurried over to it and lifted it from the glass top. Instant disappointment. It was Emma - her friend from the picture. Even though it wasn't the call she had hoped for, she answered anyway. A friendly voice in her ear was better than the current voice she had whispering to her - the one filled with self-pity and despair.

"Hey, girl! It's me! Just checking in on you. How are you?" Emma's voice was bright and cheery. Karen couldn't help but smile at the sound of it. This is why she came round here the previous night. She knew her friend would cheer her up and - more importantly - she knew she would take her in. Just as well on both accounts really.

Karen didn't have anyone else she could turn to. Not locally enough to get to anyway. Her mum and dad had moved to Cyprus four years back and - although they'd welcome her with open arms - she couldn't afford to get there. The bank accounts were in his name and she'd been frozen out, even though she hadn't done anything to deserve such treatment. She did have siblings too. A brother and a sister. Her sister lived up in Scotland with her fella but they had their own problems. They didn't need Karen dumping her issues on them too. As for Karen's brother - they weren't close. Certainly not close enough for her to feel as though she could call him. Christmas and Easter were when they tended to see each other, unless there was a funeral to attend - and with a slowly dwindling family, those were getting few and far between now.

"You there?" Emma asked.

"I'm here."

"You okay?"

"I'm…" Karen couldn't finish the sentence. She felt her eyes well up. After all the horrible words he had for her last night, before she fled the house, it was nice to hear someone be kind to her - or at least care for her wellbeing anyway. Unfortunately though, that just made it harder for her to keep her composure. All the time someone was shouting in her face, saying this and that about her, it was easy to keep check of the emotions. A small victory in not giving them the satisfaction of seeing their words have an impact on her. But when someone was kinder, it just brought all the buried emotions to the surface.

"Listen…" Emma didn't wait for Karen to finish what she was saying. She knew it had been a stupid question to begin with. After all, had Karen been okay, she wouldn't have spent the night sleeping on her sofa. She would have spent the night at her own home, with her husband. "I've told my boss I have a doctor's appointment this afternoon so I'll be home a little earlier. Give us a chance to talk properly before Sam gets home." Sam was the man in the picture, smiling next to Emma. They had been dating for three months now, coming up to four. Although he hadn't technically moved in, he did seem to spend most of his time there - not that Sam minded.

"You don't have to," Karen already felt as though she were being a pest.

"It's fine. I want to." Emma didn't wait for Karen to argue further with her, "I have to get back now but I'll see you later okay?"

"Okay." Karen knew she wouldn't be able to change Emma's mind. Truth be told, she didn't want to. She'd be happy for the company. Happy for the conversation. Talking things through with someone else might help see things more clearly too. Help Karen understand what happened to get to this point. Five years married and it was all over.

Karen was nursing a glass of wine. She hadn't touched a drop of it. Emma had brought it home from work. She thought it a good idea to open a bottle and share it whilst discussing what had landed Karen on her couch - not that Karen was ready to share immediately. Instead they spent the last hour (or so) discussing what Emma's day had been like at work. Emma didn't mind. She knew Karen welcomed the conversation as a distraction to what had been going on in her own life. She also knew that - when she was ready - to would say what was on her mind.

And she was right…

"He's been cheating on me." Karen was looking at the floor. She was embarrassed. Unable to satisfy her own man, he'd sought sexual release in the arms of another. No woman wanted that in their relationship. At least, not when they love the man they're with which - until last night - Karen did. She loved him more than life itself and - if you asked her - would have told you she could see them growing old together. What made it worse for her, she didn't even realise this affair had been happening. It wasn't a recent thing either. Her husband - her soon-to-be ex-husband - had admitted to cheating for the past three years. They'd only been married for five! For more than half of the marriage, he had been sleeping with another woman.

"You think or you know?"

"He told me." Karen looked up at Emma. She saw the pity in her eyes. She didn't want to be pitied. It made her feel pathetic and she already felt pathetic enough.

"Who? Why? I thought everything was good between you. Last time we saw you both… When was that?"

"Mike's party."

"Yes, that's right. At Mike's party. You seemed so happy. The pair of you were laughing. You looked like the perfect couple. I even said to Sam that that was what I wanted from our relationship."

Karen laughed at the thought of someone wanted a relationship like the one she'd been in. "You might want to find a new couple to base your relationship on," she said. "He's been seeing this other woman for about three years he reckons."

"What?!"

"I didn't even suspect it. All this time. I thought everything was okay." Karen wiped a tear from her eye. "I feel so fucking stupid."

"Don't you dare. He's the stupid one for wanting to cheat on you!" Emma pointed out.

Any man would have been lucky to have Karen on his arm. She was beautiful. Long blonde hair down to her waist with the brightest blue eyes you'd ever seen. Full lips; blow-job lips is how Sam once playfully described them before getting a slap from Emma. Her body was amazing too. A size eight figure; a tiny waist and a cute little bum despite not actively doing exercise to keep the shape, much to the annoyance of some of her friends whose own weight fluctuated with every mouthful of 'bad' food they had. To hear that someone would want to cheat on her just proved to Emma that men are just never satisfied with what they have.

"Who was the other woman?" Emma asked - a rather insensitive question which, had it not been for the two glasses of wine she'd consumed, probably would have stayed in the back of her mind.

"I don't know."

"Look you're welcome to stay here for as long as you need to. I'm sorry I don't have anything other than a settee but…"

"It's fine," Karen stopped her. She was just grateful she was allowed to stay there. Especially considering Emma and Sam were still in the Honeymoon stage of their relationship; fucking at any given opportunity - no matter where they were. "You're sure it's okay? I don't want to be the way."

"You won't be. It's fine. What are friends for?"

"Thank you. I really appreciate it."

"So what do you think is going to happen at home?" Emma asked.

Karen shrugged, "I don't know. He said he wanted a divorce."

Emma didn't know what to say. She sat there for a moment, in silence, before blurting out, "You know what - you're better without him. He's clearly a fucking idiot."

Karen tried to keep her bubbling emotions in check, "I still love him."

"More fool you." Emma downed the last mouthful of wine in her glass before pouring herself another, "I'm sorry. I didn't mean that. It just angers me. He fucking cheated on you. You can do better than that. You can find someone who actually gives a shit about you instead of what you can do for them. People like that piss me off. And now he's cheated - it won't be long before he cheats again. That's one good thing you can take from this; he cheated on you, yes it sucks, but there's a good chance he'll cheat on the skank he is with now too."

Karen didn't say anything. She just sat there listening to Emma's rant. She knew she was right in everything she said. Even if the relationship was salvageable - he cheated. As soon as something else came along and turned his head - he would do it again. Once a cheat always a cheat.

"You know what you need to do?" Emma continued. Karen shook her head. "Get back on that horse so to speak. Get right back out there into the field and meet someone new. Fuck him. You start getting laid again and you'll soon forget about your prick of a husband."

"I'm not ready to do that."

"You'll never be ready until you actually do it which is why you just need to get out there."

"I don't know."

"Well it's your life but if I were you, I'd be straight out there. Hell, I'd even video it and send it to my ex just to piss him off. He might not want to be with you but I guarantee he won't want you being with anyone else. It will drive him mad."

"I can't do that." Karen wasn't the sort of woman who found it easy just to go out and have sex with a stranger. Unlike Emma who - growing up - had a reputation as being a little easy (not that she minded), Karen preferred to only sleep with people she actually cared about. As it stood her husband - need to stop calling him that - was only the second person she had ever slept with. The first person was someone from her college who'd she been going out with for a good few months before finally sleeping with them. He was her first just as she was his.

"I probably would have already done it," Emma laughed. She looked up to the front door of her apartment as a key slid into the lock. "Sam's here," she said.

"You don't mind me staying?" Karen double-checked before Sam came in.

"Of course I don't mind!" Emma said. "Stop worrying about that..."

"Worrying about what?" Sam walked into the living room, dropping a full black refuse sack against the corner of the room.

"Karen thinks she is in the way here," Emma told him. No secrets between this couple. "Hey, baby."

"Hey yourself." He walked over to Emma, leaned down and gave her a kiss - a little peck. He turned to Karen, "Your Emma's best friend! She'd probably prefer it if you moved in over me," he reassured her with a cheesy grin. Karen smiled. Sam wasn't an ugly bloke by any stretch of the imagination but - at the same time - he wasn't the best looking either. The only good thing he had going for him was his laid back attitude and calming personality but - even with that - Karen genuinely believed Emma would have been bored of him by now and back on the market looking for someone with a little edge to them. "Anyone want a cup of tea? I'm parched."

"Yes please." Karen set her glass of wine to one side having taken all of three sips from it. Sam nodded and walked through to the kitchen. The two girls listened as he filled the kettle.

"You're not drinking?" Emma looked at the wasted alcohol.

"I'm sorry - I don't think I'm in the mood."

Emma paused for a while and shrugged, "More for me then!"

"Hey, Em, I brought you your clothes back that you left round mine. They're in the black bag! Sorry I didn't have anything a little more glamorous to put them in!"

"Thank you," she called back, "I'll put them away later." She turned back to Karen, "You definitely not drinking that?" Karen responded by pushing the glass across the table, towards Emma. "Shame to waste it."

III

Another morning and still no contact from her husband. Karen was sitting on the sofa staring at her phone, almost willing it to ring. She'd just made a phone call herself. A quick call to work to tell them she wouldn't be in again. They were being understand enough even if they didn't know the truth. She had told them she had a sickness bug. Working in a food environment, they were the ones who told her not to come in. They couldn't risk her passing it onto the customers. It just seemed easier to lie than tell the truth. When everything was one hundred percent definite, then she would confess and hope that they were understanding then too. At the moment she didn't even have her belongings out of the house. He had told her he wanted a divorce, they had argued and then she'd fled to Emma's. The last thing she wanted to do was tell people they were splitting up only for him to beg her to go back a little while later. People are quick to judge in this day and age and if they were to try again, at their relationship, the last thing she needed was people getting involved telling her she was making a mistake. As Emma pointed out, once a cheat - always a cheat!

It did pose the question, something Karen hadn't really thought about until now, would she accept him back in her life if he asked? Could she forgive him for sleeping with another woman? It kind of made it easier not knowing who it was. At least when she closed her eyes and saw him with another woman - the sexual encounters playing through in her head - she only really saw him as opposed to him with another person. It sounded weird but if she knew who it was - or even what they looked like - then when she pictured the scene, she would have seen their face all the time too. Only seeing her husband's meant it was easier to picture herself with him instead. Turn it from a thought of him cheating to a thought of him being intimate with her.

She dialled 1-2-1 on her mobile and pressed it against her ear. A ringing tone and then the handset connected to her voicemail. She'd had a sudden panic that she had missed his call and - for some reason - it hadn't registered. Perhaps when she was in a blackspot for the network provider? The caller would have gone straight through to answering machine. Or not. An automated voice told her there were no waiting messages. She hung up and put the phone down on the coffee table, disappointed.

"Okay - keep yourself busy, girl. That's how you beat this. Keep yourself busy so you can't think about it!" she said, standing up. She started looking around the apartment for things to clean up and noticed Emma hadn't put the bag of clothes away that Sam had brought in yesterday. A good a place as any to start.

She walked over and picked the bag up. Heavy. Struggling, she took it through to the bedroom where she dumped it on the bed before opening the wardrobe.

"Someone's been spending," she said to herself, half-jealous, as she noticed the designer clothes all hanging in a long row; dress after dress - mostly still with tags on. Karen used to be the same when it came to shopping; she'd go out on a weekend and come home with bags of clothes that she couldn't live without yet knew she'd never likely wear. A sudden thought in her head - maybe when she goes home to collect her bits, she'll be able to get the unworn stuff refunded now? Probably been over twenty-eight days but surely with the tags still on it will be okay? She sighed. Probably not. Shops are fussier these days.

The rows of clothes stretched from one end of the wardrobe to the other so Karen squashed them up together in order to fit in whatever might have been in the plastic bag. Not much room but hopefully not much from the bag will be needed to be hung. Only one way to find out.

She turned to the bag and ripped into it before tipping the contents onto the made-up bed. She stopped in her tracks, a frown on her face, and then she started to blush. A pile of clothes had fallen from the bag but not clothes Karen had expected. She had presumed there'd be a couple of tops, maybe some jeans - that kind of thing. Not this. A shining latex dress, latex panties missing their crotch, gloves and stockings - both also made from latex - and a pair of spiked heels.

"Kinky," she muttered to herself. She held the latex dress up and looked at it, unsure of what to think. On the one hand she couldn't help but feel it was a little perverted but - the other hand - definitely kinky. A little naughty? She giggled like a school girl before setting the dress to one side and exploring the other items. "Hope they've been washed," she said, seeing the crotchless panties there. A quick glance around the room and she grabbed a hairbrush from the make-up table in the corner of the room. Using the handle, she lifted the potential dirty underwear from the bed before chucking it into the wash basket, situated next to the door of on the en-suite bathroom. Even if they had been washed, it wouldn't hurt to give them another go through the washing machine. Washing machine? These things even go in the washing like conventional clothes? Karen didn't have a clue. The dress - for what it was worth - looked clean enough to hang up and she couldn't tell whether the other bits had been worn either so was happy to put them away too. One thing was for sure, this was a whole new side to her friend. A side she'd simply have to ask about when she got home. After all, there was little point in pretending not to have seen the stuff now she'd ripped into the bag to put the stuff away for Emma.

Emma should have been the one blushing but she wasn't. It was Karen who was red in the face, confessing what she saw in the bag. Emma was just laughing.

"It's a club we go to," Emma confessed. "You have to wear the appropriate clothing or you don't get in."

"A club? Like a sex club?"

"No. A nightclub. Well…" she hesitated.

"It's a sex club, isn't it? Are you two swingers?" Karen wasn't disappointed in her friend. She had no right to be. If that was the life she wanted to lead than it was entirely up to her. No one else had a right to get involved. She was just shocked because - all these years as friends - she had never suspected it and yet she thought they talked about everything together.

Emma laughed, "No we're not swingers. It's not like that. It's a proper club with various floors. Some floors have different shows on them at varied times throughout the night - like Burlesque, for example. You have a floor that's a dedicated nightclub area. You have fantasy rooms…"

"Fantasy rooms?"

Emma laughed again, "Yes. Like a room that's made to look like a hospital room for medical play."

"Medical play?"

Emma continued, "A room that's made up to look like a dungeon for those who like a little spanking and whatnot…"

"Do I dare ask?"

"I don't go in that room. And then - of course - you have the couples room."

"What the hell is a couples room?" Karen's shock continued to grow.

"Where you can - you know - get it on with your partner."

"That's weird."

"It's fun." Emma explained, "You go in there, there are beds and things around the room - you can just get down and dirty with your partner whilst other couples do the same around you." She laughed once more, "I've had some great experiences in those rooms…"

"What do you mean?"

"Well I might as well tell you - if anything it will just be funny to see your expression." Emma continued, "When you're in there - other couples can approach you and ask to join in…"

"Oh my God." Karen's mouth fell open and her eyes went wide. Emma laughed.

"One in the mouth, one in…"

"Okay that's enough. Oh my God. I can't believe you."

"And there was this time a woman approached me."

"You've shocked me."

"Why? It's all good fun. Play safe, stay safe."

"I never knew…"

"It's not something we boast about. Had I thought it would be your thing - I'd have invited you both down there," Emma said. "Somehow I can't picture your husband in that sort of environment!"

Karen's expression changed immediately and she went quiet.

"You're not still missing him? Come on, I told you, he's a dick. You can do so much better."

"No, it's not that."

"Then what is it?"

"One of the things he said to me - I wasn't adventurous enough in bed."

Emma frowned, "What kind of crazy things did he want you to do?" She suddenly looked horrified, "Oh God - he didn't want you to shit on him did he?'

"What? God - no!"

"Piss? Spit on each other?"

"No! Nothing like that!" Karen felt her face flush once more. "Okay so he wanted to tie me up once but I didn't want to."

"What? Why not? It can be great fun! You're all tied down, unable to move, and your man teases you for what feels like hours. I get wet just thinking about it," she laughed.

"You're so crude!" Karen was shocked with this side of Emma but still laughed.

"Honestly - it's amazing. Fair enough - not all the time but... So what else? He didn't cheat on you just because of that surely?"

"No. I feel stupid... Okay... He wanted me to go down on him and - after an experience I had at college - I just don't like it!"

"You don't perform oral for your husband?" It was Emma's turn to be shocked. To her, oral - either giving or receiving - was an important part of foreplay. And sometimes, when the painters were in town, it was all that was on the menu for her other half and she'd be only too happy to oblige - so long as her stomach cramps weren't too bad that is. "But that can be fucking incredible. You have all the power in that position and just hearing the guy's moans can be a turn-on…" She changed the subject, "What the hell happened at college to put you off giving head for life?"

"The guy was rough. Like he was trying to ram it down into my stomach. I actually threw up over him…"

Emma laughed.

"… Don't - it's embarrassing."

"I'm sorry. What did he do?"

"He wanted to carry on!"

"So you were doing something right then!" Emma laughed again. "You actually threw up on him?"

"Down his trousers, over his cock…. It went everywhere."

Still laughing, "Where were you?"

"We were in his bedroom. He was standing by the end and I was kneeling… He just grabbed my head and suddenly rammed his erection down my throat! I gagged, spluttered and then threw up!"

"That is the best sex story I think I have ever heard."

"Please don't repeat it."

"I can't promise that. It's too good not to share if and when the time arises. But - tell you what - to save you further embarrassment, I will leave your name out of it."

Sarcastically, "What a true friend you are."

"Even so," Emma composed herself, "a man needs head occasionally. I mean, I'm not saying it is grounds to cheat on someone but…"

"You are saying that, aren't you?"

"I don't like cheats but if a man isn't getting something at home and someone else offers it on a plate, I'm sure most would struggle to turn it down. I'm not saying they would definitely go out and cheat but - for a split second at least, they'd be tempted. And over something so simple as giving a little head? I mean, you don't have to go down on them and take the load in your mouth or anything like that but… At least go down for a few minutes. Then, once it's not and wet with your saliva and you can hear his breathing has changed to the point of sounding like he is going to cum - you can finish him by hand. No sperm in the mouth, no spit or swallow decision… And no man tempted by some cheap whore offering to do what their wife won't." She laughed, "Besides - never mind the men thinking they're missing out - you are too. The power you have when doing that, you can get a man to agree to anything when you have your mouth around their penis."

Karen laughed.

"You opened my wardrobe - you saw the clothes… Most of that was agreed with on the promise of head."

Karen laughed, "So you're a prostitute now as well?"

Emma shook her head, "Not at all. I'm an opportunist. Prostitutes get money." She changed the conversation back to Karen, "You need to come to that club."

"What?"

"You need to come with me. It's every Friday night - not that we go every Friday - and I honestly think it would do you some good to see what happens in there…"

"I'm not sure."

"I won't take no for an answer."

"Ah ha! I can't go. I don't have the clothes. You said you need to be dressed in suitable clothing and - well - I don't have any or the means to buy it so, sorry…

Maybe next time."

"It wouldn't be the first time you've borrowed my clothes," Emma winked at her, "I have more than just the outfit you saw and…"

"I'm not borrowing your crotchless knickers!"

"And… as I was saying before you interrupted me… some of it has never been worn. Still in the packaging." Emma paused a moment. "I'm not taking no for an answer," she repeated, "it will be good for you… And your fear of throwing up can be cured too."

"I don't even want to hear what you're about to suggest…"

"In the couples' room - there's these doors with locks on…"

"Why do I get the feeling I'm not going to like this?"

"The lady goes in one and the man goes in another. Between the two rooms is a wall…"

"Obviously."

"With a circular hole cut in it."

"I dread to think."

"The man pushes himself through. The woman pleasures him in any way she sees it."

"So you expect me to not only go to this club - where I'll be out of my comfort zone anyway - but you also want me to fuck a stranger."

"No. Not at all." Emma laughed, "I want you to blow him."

Karen didn't say anything for a moment. She was sitting there, her mouth still slightly agape - unsure of what to say. She thought she knew Emma but she never suspected this side from her. She knew she was adventurous and enjoyed a sex life but not to this extent!

V

Karen, Emma and Sam were sitting around the dining room table eating the fish and chips that Sam had brought in with him. He was busy waffling about this and that from his day - nothing of any real importance or interest which is probably why neither Emma nor Karen were listening to him. Emma was staring at Karen - almost willing her to look up from looking down to her dinner plate. Karen knew she was looking and - more specifically - why she was looking.

"Forget it!" Karen said - suddenly - putting her fork down and looking across to her friend who was grinning like an idiot. Sam stopped speaking immediately and looked at Karen, unsure of why there was (to him) a sudden outburst. "It's not happening."

"You need this!" Emma said.

"No. Really. I don't."

"What's going on?" Sam asked.

"It seems that whilst we were out of the house - my little friend here went snooping around the apartment."

"What? I didn't go snooping." Karen turned to Sam, "I was tidying up and went to put the clothes away you brought in yesterday."

"Ah." Sam already knew where this was heading.

"She's coming with us on Friday!" Emma blurted out excitedly.

"I'm not!" She turned back to Sam, "She wants me to fuck a stranger…"

"Blow!" Emma corrected her. "She has this thing with giving head."

"You said you wouldn't say anything!" Karen shot Emma a filthy look.

"It's Sam. I can tell Sam. That's fair game."

"A thing with giving head? What's that - love it and looking for some more?" Sam was grinning like an idiot now.

Karen sighed, "What? No. Eww…"

"She doesn't like it because of a bad experience…"

"What experience?" Sam asked.

"It doesn't matter!" Karen shot Emma another look who - in turn - gave Sam a look as though to tell him she would explain later.

"She thinks it will be a good idea to blow a stranger to get over my fear of giving head," Karen explained before Emma made it worse for her.

Emma explained her line of thinking to Sam, "She can use the Glory Hole.."

"Glory Hole?" Karen raised an eyebrow.

"That's what they call it," Emma explained. She continued, "That way she keeps control of how much she takes into her mouth. A man can't push it down her throat when there is a wall between the two of them…"

"True."

"I'm not blowing a stranger. Have you heard of STDs?"

"Have you heard of protection?" Emma answered back.

"Oh good, a mouthful of rubber."

"I have some strawberry flavoured ones. Welcome to take a couple. Taste pretty good," Sam piped up.

"Sam, I don't even want to know how you would know that."

He laughed as he realised how that had sounded. "Emma told me."

"I don't know what he's talking about. I've never tried them," Emma winked at Karen, purposefully winding Sam up.

"Fuck you!" Sam's tone was playful, not aggressive. He knew what Emma was trying to do.

"I'm not blowing a stranger!" Karen shouted above the two as they flirted back and fourth.

"You don't have to. Remember Nick?"

"Nick?" Karen looked at her friend with a raised eyebrow.

"He was at the Christmas party I had here."

Karen thought back to the party. That was half a year ago now and she could barely remember a thing, especially with the amount she'd had to drink that night. She shook her head, "I don't remember."

"Well you were loved up at the time with hubby but you noticed Nick because you asked me who he was... Before the conversation really took off, your husband came back from the toilet..."

"I don't remember."

Emma could tell by Karen's face that she did remember. She had liked Nick and for good reason too. He was handsome in a rugged-kind of way. Dark, longish hair, dark eyes, heavy stubble and a good body hidden beneath his various designer suits he wore for work. A man who was single because his work didn't leave much time for socialising - he was a perfect rebound for Karen. A little bit of fun but nothing serious. And - what made him even better for her - he had noticed her at the party too...

"I'm taking you to the club on Friday and Sam can bring Nick. We can meet down there and you two can go into the Glory Hole room... You can get reacquainted with a love for giving head and start to forget about your asshole husband... Come on! Life is for living. You only live once!"

"I'm not doing it."

"It's harmless fun!"

"It's not who I am!"

"And that's why your marriage failed! Come on, live a little! Be adventurous!" Emma blurted out. Karen immediately went quiet. "I'm sorry. I don't know why I said that. That was unfair and cruel. I'm sorry. Your marriage failed because your husband was a dick. I'm sorry."

"It's fine…"

"No, I crossed a line. I was just getting over-excited…"

"Honestly, it's fine."

"Just come to the club with us on Friday," Sam piped up, "it's a good laugh. You don't have to go into any of the sexual orientated rooms. It's not all like that. It genuinely is a blast with people who are letting their hair down."

Karen looked at Sam and then back to Emma. "Okay. I'll go. But I'm not going into any rooms with holes in it or where people might be having sex. Deal?"

Emma smiled, "Deal."

"As you say, we only live once, hey." She took a sip from her drink.

"So… We best find an outfit that you like then!"

"And I'm not borrowing any of your crotchless clothing line!" Karen laughed.

"I promise you, you won't regret this. Even if you aren't into the riskier side of what the venue has to offer - the rest of it is just as good. Everyone is so laid back there. It's not like your usual club with pissed up idiots hell bent on ruining it for you."

"To be honest, I just want to get out and - as you said - I need to be a little more adventurous. Might as well jump in at the deep end and - before you say it -

the club by itself is the deep end. What you were suggesting earlier doesn't even have a bottom to it!"

Emma laughed, "Soon as you've finished dinner, we'll find something good for you to wear." She turned to Sam, "And you have to wait in the living room!"

"Ah come on, I'll see it Friday anyway!" Sam moaned.

"Well?" Emma asked.

She was standing next to Karen. Both of them in front of the full length mirror in Emma's bedroom. Behind them - on the bed - was a mountain of fetish wear. PVC, leather and latex. Emma wasn't kidding around when she said she had more of it. Some of it - as she also admitted - hadn't even come out of the wrapping yet; naughty little outfits Sam had purchased for her because he wanted to see her in them even though she hadn't had the time to model all of them for him yet.

Karen was standing in a skin-tight catsuit made from latex. It was a grey colour although some of it looked to be transparent - especially around the nipples. A zip ran from the front of the crotch around the under carriage. A second zip on the back - running the same line as the first zipper - went from top to bottom. Easy access depending on which way your partner wanted to go in.

The catsuit was a struggle to get in. It really was skin-tight showing all of Karen's curves. She was baffled how Emma would get into it if she struggled. Although not much bigger than Karen, she was still bigger and every extra inch would have been a squeeze to cover up.

"It's tight," Karen pointed out the obvious.

"But it feels good, right?"

Karen moved her body a little; arching her back slightly, bending forwards a little, stretching up with her arms and then down again - the latex material gripped her firmly and refused to release her; no movement from her skin whatsoever.

"It kind of does," Karen giggled. She couldn't believe she was standing here dressed head to foot in latex. If she were to dress up for the bedroom, it was usually pretty knickers made from silk - a matching bra to boot. She always thought latex was for whores or porn stars, of which she was neither. "I like it," she admitted.

"I knew you would. I remember the first time I wore it. Sam had bought it for me. He loves all things latex. He likes the shine and the general feel against his skin…"

"Okay - don't need to know anymore!" Karen laughed again.

"I put it on for him and - from that moment - I've been hooked on it. When he suggested the club I was like you - a little unsure - but, honestly, I love it there and some of the people look absolutely stunning in their outfits. I swear some of them think it is more of a fashion show than a nightclub but that's what makes it all the more amazing to see."

Karen couldn't take her eyes off of her form in the mirror. The first time for as long as she could remember she felt sexy. More than that, she felt a little naughty - not wanting to take the outfit off.

"You sure you don't mind me borrowing it?"

"Not at all. I have this sexy little dress that I want to wear."

"Show me?"

Emma walked over to the wardrobe and opened it. Hanging at the back, behind some other clothes, was a red latex dress. The bottom of the dress had clips hanging down which Karen presumed attached to stockings of some description. The dress itself, short enough to just about cover the buttocks.

"Put it on!" Karen urged her.

"Okay." Emma laid it on the bed and stripped her jeans and top off. Whilst she started to slide the rubber dress over her body, Karen turned back to the mirror and checked herself out again.

"I feel like I've been missing out," she said - running her hands down the front of her body.

"Whether you want to or not, you're going to turn some heads in that. You look amazing."

"I feel amazing!"

Karen's life was a mess. Her husband was still leaving her and she didn't have anywhere to live but right now - in this moment - she didn't care. Much to her own surprise, she was having fun.

"Can you do me up?" Emma had her back to Karen. The dress was on but her back exposed due to the zip being down to the base of her spine. Karen did as requested and zipped her friend into the equally tight-fitting dress. Once zipped in, Emma pulled the bottom down, ensuring the material wasn't wrinkled anywhere. Satisfied, she turned to Karen. "What do you think?"

"Put the rest on," said Karen, noticing the clips for the stockings hanging down Emma's legs. Emma didn't need to be told twice. She opened up a drawer, at the other end of the room, and pulled out a pair of stockings; the same red as the dress. Karen watched as Emma greased her legs up with a handful of the special oil; sold with the latex outfit and supposedly the best to use as it didn't burn through the rubber. Whilst Emma started to slide herself into the latex stockings she explained that - although fairly tough - the material was easy to ruin if you used the wrong product on it. She clipped the bottom of the dress to the stockings and stood up.

"What do you think?"

"It looks hot."

Much like the catsuit did with Karen's figure, the dress accentuated Emma's own frame - even enhancing the breasts which - with thanks to the cut of the dress - were showing off a good cleavage.

"My hair in pig-tails I reckon and a pair of heels to match!" Emma was excited to be wearing the outfit. She had already tried it on once but getting in it again just made her think about what could potentially happen at the club. Unlike Karen, she had no reservations about going into the couple's room. In fact, it was the reason she wanted to go! "What do you think? Should we give Sam a glimpse of what he can expect?"

Karen giggled, "Okay."

Emma giggled too, a naughty spark in her eye, "Hey, Sam! Can you come here a minute?" She walked over next to Karen and put her arm around her, twisting her friend round so that they were both facing the closed bedroom door. The door handle turned and Sam pushed the door open, stepping into the room. Immediately his mouth fell open - his eyes pinned to the two girls.

"Fucking hell!"

"We just thought you might want to see what we have lined up for Friday." Emma teased. Sam took a step towards the girls, his arms outstretched towards Emma. Quickly she stepped forward and pushed him back out of the room. "Oh no. No touching. I told you, this is just a glimpse. You can touch on Friday!" She laughed as she slammed the door shut on him. "I hope you're ready because that's how people are going to be looking at you on Friday!" she said with a wink - a cheeky grin on her face.

"I feel fucking great!" Karen said. She couldn't stop running her hands down the shiny material.

"Ooh the good girl swearing... I have awakened a monster..."

Karen ignored her, "If you were to bring your friend to the club... You think..." Her face suddenly flushed, "Never mind."

"No. What? You want me to call Nick up?" Emma's face lit up even more than it already was. "I'll call him. I know he will want to go! Especially when I mention your name."

Karen buried her head in her hands, hiding from Emma, "I can't believe I'm doing this... Okay... " She looked up to Emma, "Okay... Call him! No... Wait..."

"Too late. I'm calling him!"

"I can't do this!" Karen was just talking for the sake of it. In her mind, she was already imagining how Friday could play out and - despite how she initially felt - she was excited. Genuinely excited. "This has to be our secret though!" Karen suddenly said.

"Fine."

"And can I use some of those strawberry flavoured..."

"Definitely!" Emma cut her off mid-sentence.

A huge, naughty smile suddenly spread across Karen's flushed face. Emma was grinning too. Having been in this position before herself, she knew the ride Karen was about to take and it was wild. Not just that but it was freeing too. It let you forget about normal rules for a while. It made you feel alive and gave you an adrenaline buzz normal life didn't usually dish up. It was an eye-opener.

Karen, Emma and Sam were waiting for the taxi to collect them. All of them were dressed ready to impress at the club. Karen was in the catsuit, Emma was in the red rubber dress and Sam was wearing leather trousers and a black latex top with a cuff - heavy-duty black boots on his feet.

Karen had been looking forward to it all week - especially after Nick agreed to come along and be Karen's willing partner - but now she was getting anxious. Cold feet were definitely setting in - not that Emma was about to let her back out.

"It's fine to be nervous, it's new to you. But I promise - once you get there - have a few drinks, everything will be fine."

"What if he doesn't like me when we meet? What if he has changed his mind since he last saw me? It was a good few months ago."

"Don't be stupid. You're stunning - inside and out - why would he change his mind?"

"I just..."

Emma cut her off, "You've got the condoms Sam gave you?"

Karen ignored her and asked a question of her own, "Okay - what if I change my mind? What if I don't like him now?"

"This is all about a release for you. Emotionally and sexually. We'll get there, have a couple of drinks and then you can go into the room and wait for him to come in. You don't even have to see him first. Afterwards, if you want, you can face him..."

Karen blushed, "Not sure I'll be able to!"

"… Or you can sneak off back to the club area where Sam and I will be dancing the night away…"

"We're not going in the couples' room?" Sam looked disappointed.

"Let's just let Karen do what she needs to do first, honey. Try not to be selfish." A car horn sounded from outside in the street. "That'll be the taxi. Ready?"

"Why don't you two just go without me? I'm not sure I am ready for this yet."

"You've been looking forward to it since you first slid into that outfit!" Emma was right, Karen had been excited for the evening. It was just the uncertainty of it all that was putting her off now. The unfamiliarity of it all. "You'll be fine when you've had a couple more drinks!" Karen had already had two glasses of wine whilst getting ready. Clearly it was going to take more than that for her to loosen up. "If you don't come, you'll only regret it."

"I just think - somethings might be better left to fantasy?"

"Not a chance. Get your bag, we're leaving!" Emma physically turned Karen around and pushed her towards the front door.

Sam laughed, "Everything will be fine!" He reassured Karen, "I'll keep an eye on you all night, make sure you don't get any unwanted attention."

Emma shot him a suspicious look, "We all know what part of her you'll be keeping an eye on! You just behave yourself!"

"I wasn't doing anything!" Sam protested his innocence but Emma knew him well and had already seen him checking out Karen's latex-clad rear, not that she could blame him. It did look amazing in that catsuit. She didn't mind Sam window-shopping so long as he didn't enter the shops, so to speak. Emma opened the door and ushered both Karen and Sam out - starting with Sam, giving him less chance to window-shop. Grabbing her bag from the floor she followed the others out and closed the door.

Karen was sitting in the back of the taxi with Emma. Sam was in the front, with the driver.

"Yeah, yeah, I know the club. Can't say I've ever been though."

Emma and Sam were talking to the driver, explaining (lying) that nothing untoward happened in the club despite its reputation. It was just a normal club, the only difference being in what people wore inside. They didn't really care if they believed them or not, both of them stifling their laughter. They were used to people like the taxi driver giving them the look up and down - judging them, or perving at them. Karen was less used to it though and felt self-conscious, especially as she kept catching the taxi-driver's eye when he glanced at her via the car's rear-view mirror.

"Well you're all looking good!" Another glance at Karen, using the mirror.

"So what did you want to do then?" Emma asked. She was looking at Karen, not that she noticed. Karen had turned to looking out of the window in an effort to stop catching the taxi driver's eye. "Karen!" She got Karen's attention.

"I'm sorry?"

"What did you want to do?"

"About what?"

"Nick!" Emma continued, "Did you want to meet him in the bar first?"

"I'm really not sure about this."

"Come on - you were looking forward to it the other day," Sam piped up from the front.

"Uh oh - this your first time going in?" the taxi-driver joined in too.

Karen looked at Emma, "Can we talk about this another time?" She discreetly nodded towards the driver - a signal she hoped Emma would pick up on. It was one thing to go to a club with other people in similar clothes, with similar likes... It was another thing entirely to openly discuss the evening's plans with a complete stranger who didn't even seem to appreciate the club, let alone the 'rumours' he had heard about it.

Emma laughed and leaned forward into the front of the taxi, "So it's my friends first time going to the club and she's nervous. She is meeting someone there..."

"Emma!" Karen's face flushed and - suddenly - her body felt a lot hotter in the latex than it had done previously. She pulled her friend back onto the seat.

"You're a very pretty girl," the taxi driver stated, "I'm sure the man will like you." He had jumped to the conclusion that Karen was nervous about meeting a new date. Karen was fine with that.

"Thank you."

"So - did you want to meet him at the bar first or..."

"I don't know..." Karen felt harassed and it was making her want to turn around and go home more and more now.

"A drink is always good," the taxi-driver spoke out again - much to the amusement of Emma, "helps you relax. Just make sure you don't go leaving it unattended. Hear all sorts on the television these days; people slipping things into drinks... Like a horror story every day you pick up anything related to the news."

Sam leaned round from the front. In his hand was a silver hip-flask, "Here you go. And - don't worry - nothing slipped inside... Well... Nothing other than the whiskey." He flashed Karen a wink. She didn't hesitate. She unscrewed the cap and took a swig - coughing as soon as she swallowed it down; the liquor burning all the way down to the pit of her nervous stomach.

"You can't take that in with you!" Emma snatched the flask away from Karen, sniffing the contents as she did so. "Whiskey? Really?" Karen handed her the screw-cap.

"They won't care I have it. By the time we get there, it will be empty!" Sam laughed.

"You're unbelievable!" Before she put the cap back on, she took a swig herself. Unlike Karen, she didn't cough. She put the lid on and handed it back to Sam who - again - removed the cap and took a swig.

"Can I get me some of that?" the driver asked with a cheeky laugh.

"Err, maybe when we get out of the car!" Emma said from the back.

"Sam, can you pass me the flask?" Karen asked. She didn't have to meet up with Nick if she didn't want to. Well maybe meet him for a drink but - she didn't have to go into the couples room with him. No one could force her to do that. If it happened, it was her decision. But even meeting Nick, taking that room out of the equation, made her nervous. She hadn't met a man for a date, or anything else, for years. That and the fact Emma was never going to let her back out of going to the club now she'd come this far - she suddenly found herself desperate to get drunk enough to go in and enjoy herself. Sam took another swig for himself and happily passed the flask to the rear of the vehicle.

"So - bar first or did you just want to go straight for it?" Emma pushed. She shook her head, "Actually don't answer that. You're going straight in. Less opportunity for you to back out."

"I'm really not sure…"

"Have another swig. Flask needs to be empty before we get there!" Just as Karen realised she wasn't going to be able to get out of going into the club, Emma knew she'd need to be drunk (or even tipsy) first or else it just wouldn't happen. Maybe it wasn't such a bad idea, Sam bringing the hip flask.

"Save me some! Glass of red I had with lunch didn't even touch the side!"

Sam looked over to the taxi-driver. Looking at him, and the smile on his face, he could no longer tell if the man was joking, or not. Thankfully - for their safety - the club was close; only a few corners away.

Heavy clubland music pumped through the rooms of the club. Karen was looking around - a deer caught in headlight - as Emma and Sam led her through the corridors. It was early - just gone ten in the evening - and the place was heaving with people wearing a mix of outfits; all of them looking stunningly attractive, most in latex, some in burlesque and a handful in nothing but paint. Both Emma and Sam were grinning from ear to ear; Sam leading Emma slightly, who had a hold of Karen's hand.

"It's incredible, isn't it?" Emma was smiling at Karen.

Karen smiled at her, unsure of what to say. There was no denying the outfits were incredible. The music, shaking the walls, was tolerable - pretty much standard club music; heavy bass with an unknown female vocalist singing over the top of the repeated tune. Even so, and despite the alcohol, Karen still wasn't one hundred percent comfortable.

Another corridor.

A room on the left did nothing to cure Karen's fears. She glanced in and there - leaning over a wooden horse with his arse up in the air, wearing nothing but a latex gimp mask - a man was being spanked by a woman wearing a similar outfit to Karen. Her weapon of choice seemingly being a table tennis bat.

"That's the dungeon area!" Emma shouted out over the music. "Whipping, spanking, restraints… All goes on in there if you fancy trying it. I was once strapped to this large cross. Had a pretty girl hit me with a leather flogger. I think I enjoyed it?" She laughed, "I might have to try again to be sure." She continued,

"There's also these thrones in there. You sit down and put your feet up on these stools... Before you know it - you're surrounded by gimps all willingly massaging the soles of your feet and your toes. Pretty relaxing actually..."

They walked on.

Karen couldn't see how it could be relaxing. Sure, on occasion, a foot massage could be quite nice. She could see that. But would it really be relaxing having gimps fight over touching your feet? And did they expect anything back? They give a good enough massage, as a thank you - you pay them with a well earned hand job? Was that how it worked here? She shuddered at the thought.

The next room.

A large room that looked like a television-set. Specifically it looked like it was from a hospital drama; white walls, white floors - sterile, all clean. A hospital bed with a thick, black leather mattress that looked somewhat out of place. A girl laying upon it, naked. She was writhing around at the touch of a group of latex nurses around her - standing with an authentic looking doctor; a tall man pressing various medical equipment against the 'patients' skin, causing her to sigh and groan in pleasure. Two of the three nurses looked up to the door - straight at Karen. They beckoned for her to come in, with a smile and a wink. She shook her head.

"If you can let yourself go and really surrender yourself - that room is something else entirely," Emma laughed. "All these hands exploring your body and some of the equipment used..." She laughed again. "Wow."

"It looks like a hospital!"

"That's the point. A common fetish - doctors and nurses."

Karen walked on. Emma and Sam walked with her.

"There's no real experiments going on in there... Well... Other than finding out what makes you climax… Trust me…. You let yourself go and you'll cum in ways you never knew imaginable."

Karen knew there must have been some truth in what Emma was saying. If there wasn't, why would she have spent so much money on the outfits? And why would she keep going back? Besides - the thought of being on that bed, despite the medical surroundings, with all those people touching her, with the sole aim to make her orgasm… It was sexy. Naughty, yes, but definitely sexy.

Sam stopped by another room. The door was closed. He looked over to Emma. Karen was her friend. He only knew her through association. That wasn't to say he didn't like her, because he did, but Emma was the one who really knew her. She was the one - other than Karen - who would be able to say whether this was a good idea or not; whether her friend was really ready for what lay on the other side of the door. Emma recognised the look and nodded.

"We're here then!" Sam said. His tone was awkward. He looked over to Emma again for help. This was her idea - she was the one who needed to take Karen through this.

Emma jumped in, "This is the couple's room…"

On the other side of the door there'd be couples engaged in consensual sex on beds - and other furniture such as chairs - scattered around the room. Some would be engaged on full-on fucking, others would be performing fellatio. Some people would even be standing at the sides, watching - some of them masturbating, some of the others wishing they could be a part of it. There were two other rooms in the far corner, to the left, next to each other. The door on the left had a sign showing it was for the ladies. There was a sign on the door to the right showing it was for gentlemen. There were locks on both doors so the people inside could not be disturbed. A warning - pinned to the wall on the left - warning people not to swap rooms, no doubt put there after a homosexual man went into the ladies' room and blew an unsuspecting straight guy who was expecting the soft lips of a woman.

Emma realised she was putting her best friend in a difficult situation and - despite the way she'd been pushing her into this - she gave Karen a way out, "You've come to the club, that's good enough. If you don't want to do this - you don't have to. I'll tell Nick plans have changed…"

Karen suddenly looked over her shoulder and then over Sam's shoulder, "Is he here?"

"He is. I've had a text. He's in the bar. If you want to go there first - have a drink with him - you can. If you don't want to come back here, you don't have to. He's a nice guy. If he wasn't I wouldn't have suggested he came. If you want to go home after a drink, he'll be fine with that."

Karen took a deep breath. The effects of the alcohol had hit just before she came to the club, much to her relief. It certainly made it easier for her to walk over the threshold. "I want to see in there," she nodded towards the door. She thought for a moment, her mind replaying the scene from the medical room - the pleasure that woman seemed to be having. That could be her. Maybe not in that particular scene but another situation… The one being organised by Emma. It could be amazing and - if it wasn't - then tomorrow would be another day and this whole evening would be something put to the back of the mind and never repeated. "Maybe you should text him and tell him to come down?" She smiled nervously.

Emma grinned, "You're going to do this?"

Karen's husband was fucking someone else, why shouldn't she have some fun? And - his words were still stuck in her mind; she wasn't adventurous… She might not be yet but - tonight - she could become so. This was the first - albeit strange - step to become more sexually liberated. The more she thought about it, the more she heard the woman screaming out an orgasm down the corridor, the more she wanted this.

"I am!" she said.

"And you've got the condoms?" Karen had slid the condoms between her cleavage. They were kept from falling out by the way the latex held her tight. She nodded to her friend who nodded back. "Well okay then! I'll text him!" She reached into her small purse and pulled out her phone. A second later and the text was sent. Less time and a reply came through - a simple smiley face. Emma grinned when she read it and then turned the phone to show her Karen. Karen's face immediately reddened.

"You might want to go and get yourself prepared," Emma beamed. "We'll wait here for him."

"We can't wait in there?" Sam nodded towards the couples' room.

"We'll wait here," Emma repeated much to Sam's disappointment.

"I feel nervous," Karen giggled.

"Remember you're in control. All the man can do is poke himself through the wall. They might be able to move a little bit but - when they're pushed right through - that's as far as they can thrust so... Keep that in mind and you won't have any college-day problems..."

"This is okay, isn't it?" A sudden doubt in Karen's mind.

"It's a bit of fun. You're not running off to get married, you're not starting a long-term relationship. You're not putting yourself at risk if you're playing safe. It's just fun." Sam answered. He knew the answer to this one.

Karen nodded, "It's going to be fun." She suddenly giggled, "Naughty."

"Get in there!" Emma urged her, "Before you change your mind!"

"Okay. This is it…" She turned to the door and just stopped as though she'd run out of batteries.

"You need to open the door to get in there!" Emma said.

Karen giggled and reached out for the handle. She turned it and walked in to the sound of men grunting, women groaning and the scent of sex hanging in the lust-filled air. Rubber, sweat, pheromones… The door closed behind her and she paused a moment, standing in the open, to allow her eyes the opportunity to adjust to the low level of light in the room. Slowly the shapes became clearer. There must have been eleven couples engaged in sexual intercourse on beds stationed around the room. Five beds in total laid out in a square with the fifth bed (a circular one) positioned in the middle. Couples were having sex in whatever space they could find on the bed; the bed in the centre filled with three couples - all going at it. One girl was on her hands and knees with a leather-clad man behind her - fucking her hard. She was staring directly at another woman who was in a similar position on the other side of the bed who was also staring back, both seemingly getting off on watching the other being fucked. On the same bed a man was sitting with his back to the other couples. A woman was standing in front of him, bent over, bouncing up and down on his covered erection as he hands explored her ass cheeks - one thumb apparently up her arse. People weren't making love in this room, they were fucking.

Realising she was a little exposed, standing out in the open, Karen backed towards the wall where she accidentally bumped into someone.

"Sorry!" she turned to see who she had collided with. A man was standing with his back to the wall. His cock was in his hands and he was pumping away furiously whilst watching the action in the room; a live sex show to get him off. He looked at Karen and licked his lips, eyeing her up and down. His mind was already picturing Karen standing behind him - reaching around, putting a hand around his neck whilst the other hand also stretched around his body and wanked him off. Karen quickly moved away from him before he made any suggestions or sprayed his seed onto her. The fact he wasn't wearing any protection also concerned her, making her wonder what exactly was underfoot.

Like the man she'd accidentally bumped into, she put her back to the wall and looked inwards to the couples. The sight of a stranger wanking himself didn't do anything for Karen but - had there been anyone there to confess it to - she would have admitted that it was quite erotic seeing couples having sex in various positions, more so due to the clothes they were wearing - tight fitting outfits that accentuated their finer features. On the bed closest to her now there was a strong-looking man in latex shorts that hug his firm arse. He was standing by the edge of the bed and you could see all the muscles working under the latex, sleeveless top that he was wearing as he held a girl's legs over his shoulders whilst drilling her hard as she laid upon her back. She was in a latex dress, the bottom of which was hitched up over her stomach giving everyone full sight of her undercarriage and the thick cock pushing in and out of her shaven, wet pussy. Long boots were laced up her model-like legs. Her face hidden by a rubber hood that she was wearing - showing only her mouth and eyes with her blonde hair poking from the top, tied in a tight pony-tail. She was screaming the loudest but given the pounding she was getting from the strong man gripping her in position, Karen couldn't blame her.

As Karen watched the couple - a part of her wishing she were in the position of the woman - another man approached them from the right. Naked, and with an erection, he climbed onto the bed and positioned himself so that he was kneeling to the side of the woman's head. As far as Karen could tell from where she was standing, no words were exchanged and yet the woman turned to the supposed stranger and slid his penis between her lips, taking him to the back of her throat with ease. The man slowly started rocking back and fourth as the woman continued sucking.

Despite never being in that situation herself, Karen found herself getting aroused.

The man she'd previously bumped into as she came in suddenly groaned out loud. Karen looked just in time to see a mess of sticky cum spurt from the tip of his uncircumcised penis. He visibly shuddered, pulled up a pair of tiny rubber looking shorts and made his exit from the room. The opening and closing of the door reminded Karen that she needed to be in the cubicle before Nick came in. Although she was unsure as to whether his face would be covered or not, she didn't want to be seen by him before going in there - a fear that he'd suddenly back out of wanting to go in with her as she was no longer what he looked for in a woman. Another fear that she too would back out, too embarrassed to go through with it.

The woman from the bed removed the cock from her mouth long enough to scream the roof down with an orgasm. Karen glanced over. The strong man was still fucking her, refusing to let up despite her whole body twitching and her back arching with the force of the climax. The man, on his knees next to her, was stroking himself - keeping the momentum going for his own orgasm whilst she regained her breath, not that the strong man was giving her much chance to. The ecstasy they were all in reminded Karen why she was doing this; to experience something she'd not done before, to broaden her own views, to become more adventurous and as a fuck you to her cheating husband. Unsure as to whether she'd ever experienced such an orgasm as the woman before her, there was no way she was backing out of anything now. She wanted a taste of what these strangers had and tonight was the night.

She turned away from them and headed for the back of the room. Two cubicles on the far one. One for the ladies, one for the men. Both doors open, waiting for a willing couple to venture in.

Karen locked the door. The cubicle was much like a changing room - similar to one you'd find in a department store. There was a hanger on the back wall, along with a long mirror. There was a small stall in there which could be sat on if so desired. The light in the cubicle was dim. Looking up there was a bulb situated between the two cubicles - hanging just above the wall that separated them. Karen's nervous mind tried to ignore the round hole cut away in the very same wall and she found herself questioning why the builders didn't see fit to put a light socket in both cubicles in order to offer more light. Without answering herself she suddenly turned and reached up for the bolt on the door that she'd previously closed, a sudden urge to pull it back and get the hell out of there. She stopped herself and took a step back until her back was against the mirror.

"You can do this," she kept telling herself again and again as her heart raced in her chest.

A door closed in the next room causing Karen to freeze.

A second later and she heard the familiar sound of a bolt sliding across, locking the door.

This was it. He was here.

She walked over to the hole in the wall and leaned down to it.

"Nick? Is that you?" she whispered through, her voice a little shaky from the nerves.

A muffled voice replied.

Karen moved away from the hole - her eyes fixed to it, unsure of what to expect. Was he going to peer through and say hello or… An erect penis slowly came through the hole. Okay, so no saying hello first. But then, if she had wanted a hello first, she would have agreed to meet him at the bar for a drink beforehand. At least, that was what she told herself.

She reached down into her cleavage and withdrew one of the rubbers. She tore into the packaging with her teeth and pulled the condom out. And then she froze again. Her eyes transfixed to the hard-on in front of her, watching it occasionally twitch in anticipation to what was coming.

Stop overthinking this, she thought to herself. She knew the longer she stayed there, staring at it, the more she would talk herself out of it. She shook her head from side to side as though trying to forget all pre-programmed responses to this situation (mainly being to run) and moved forward, closer to the cock. With a shaking hand, she slowly rolled the soft latex of the condom down the shaft. Nick groaned from the other side - a muffled groan, yes, but definitely a groan.

With the rubber on, she slowly stroked the shaft up and down - a firm grip to stop the rubber from sliding off again. Without letting go, she pulled the stool closer to where she was and took a seat. The perfect height (or not - depending on how you look at it) with the penis inches away from her face; her mouth.

"What did you expect? You're not exactly the most adventurous in the bedroom department, are you? Honestly - sometimes it's like having sex with a plank of wood. I like my partners to be a little more involved… A little more into it. You don't dress up for me, you don't give me head, most of the time you want the lights off… I'm sorry but it's boring!" Her husband's words played through her head again and again as Karen felt a bubble of anger pop inside of her. Without a second though, she moved her head forward - mouth open - and slid the covered cock into her mouth. She clamped her lips shut together, tightly, and - with one hand gripped on the shaft slowly stroking - she started moving her head backwards and forwards whilst all the time sucking, creating a nice vacuum for Nick. The strange taste of strawberry from the condom's flavouring.

From the other side of the wall she could hear muffled sighs as the man felt the tightness of her mouth around his throbbing penis. Karen didn't stop but nor could she believe she was actually doing it! More to the point, she couldn't believe she was actually enjoying it. A feeling of power at the thought of being in control of Nick's pleasure. A wetness in her pussy that had started in the other room, watching the couples fucking, and only seemed to be getting wetter now she had this man's cock in her mouth.

She suddenly released his cock from her mouth and - quickly - pulled the condom off, dropping it to the floor leaving his penis bare in front of her. The taste of the strawberry had faded quickly, leaving a disgusting taste of rubber that she didn't enjoy. Besides, she didn't need it. His cock looked clean enough. She took a hold of the shaft once more and gave it a squeeze as she pulled on it. A clear liquid dribbled from the tip. She leaned forward and - with a flick of the tongue - tasted it. A salty pre-cum. It didn't taste as bad as she thought and she wasted no time in sinking her mouth around the cock once more; her hand still working the shaft as she moved her head back and fourth. Complete control. Nick's sighs from the other side of the partition enough to egg her on.

Knowing he couldn't suddenly ram his dick down her throat, causing her to gag, Karen found that she was enjoying the whole sensation of giving head. She liked the texture of the shaft on her tongue, licking all over whilst it was in her mouth - the raised bits where the veins were, all the way to the smoothness of the head and the slight taste of salt in his pre-cum. She liked hearing his soft, barely audible moans and groans from behind the partition. She loved the fact she had the control and he was completely at her mercy. She loved it all and she wanted more. She wanted to taste him. She wanted to feel him ejaculate into her mouth. She wanted to know the texture of his spunk, the taste, the hotness… She wanted everything this situation offered for her.

She continued working the shaft with both her mouth and her hand until her jaw started to ache. Only then did she pull the cock from her mouth - not that she stopped stroking with her hand, a strong motion up and down the shaft keeping the rhythm going so as not to stop any potential build of an orgasm. Even though the penis wasn't in her mouth - it didn't stop her from using her tongue. She kept her mouth close and - with her tongue poking out - she continued licking the head with purposeful up and down flicks.

From the other side of the wall, it sounded as though Nick hit his hands against the wall - perhaps to steady himself? Karen didn't stop what she was doing - instead taking it as a sign she was doing everything just right and that he was close to the point of an orgasm. He hit the wall again and Karen couldn't help but to smile as she increased the speed her hand moved up and down his shaft. She stopped licking the tip long enough to spit some warm saliva over his cock; a lubricant to stop from chaffing him with her firm grip and a way to make the whole sensation that little bit better for him.

His groans were louder now, funny throaty noises of appreciation. He had to be close. She sunk her mouth around his cock again and sucked back, creating that vacuum once more, before sucking up and down the length of the shaft in time with the strong movements from her hand.

Another hit against the wall.

A louder groan - so clear it almost sounded as though they were in the same room.

With both her hand and her mouth she felt a strong throb from his penis and then a second and then a third and then... A strange movement from the base of the shaft... Karen quickly pointed her tongue up towards the roof of her mouth as a thick stream of spunk shot from Nick's throbbing cock. She gulped but managed to keep it collected there, underneath her tongue, without accidentally letting any shoot down the back of her throat. She was curious enough - and horny enough - to swallow it but she wanted to remain in control of it. That was the whole point of this; to experience all that was to offer.

The penis had stopped twitching and the semen had stopped shooting from the end. Karen slowly slid her mouth backwards until the cock slipped out, a sticky mess coated in both cum and spit. She lowered her tongue back down from the roof of the mouth and - with a closed mouth - scooped up Nick's deposit so that it pooled in the centre of it. A strong taste of salt with the clumpy consistency. Feeling incredibly horny, she closed her eyes and ran her hand down her body until her fingers were toying with her clitoris through the skintight latex of the catsuit and then - stroking herself hard - she swallowed down hard. The semen felt like cough syrup; a sticky feeling as it lined the sides all the way down from throat to stomach. An instant wish that there was more to guzzle. Still rubbing herself, she opened her eyes hoping the penis was still there and that there was a little cum on the verge of dripping from the end of it.

It was gone.

It didn't matter though as she felt the powerful build-up of an intense orgasm brewing. Her mind kept replaying the sensation of having the semen shoot into her mouth, the feeling of the twitching cock, the sudden taste of the salty gloop, the feeling of it running down the back of her throat.... Her whole body tensed as the orgasm hit hard. Her spare hand grabbed onto the hanger, stuck to the wall, to save herself from buckling to the floor completely. It seemed to last forever before she could catch her breath and her body stopped shuddering. Her pussy was throbbing as the remnants of the orgasm rippled through her. She laughed, having surprised herself at how easily she came.

With shaky legs she stood up, having made a mental note to thank Emma for insisting she came along. This was just a taste (literally) of what was on offer and now she was ready to experience more. Well - maybe not straight away but... Definitely over the coming months. She wanted to be the woman lying on the medical bed, she wanted to be the one tied to a cross - getting spanked in the dungeon area. She wanted to even be the one dishing out the spanking to either a man or a woman, maybe even both. She wanted a stranger inside of her, forcing her to have multiple orgasms. This one taste of this man had awakened a side she never knew existed and it was screaming to be satisfied.

Karen turned to the door and slid the bolt across. Despite the sudden yearning for all of these different sexual encounters, she still felt her face start to flush at the prospect of looking Nick in the eye. With any luck - she thought - he'd be feeling the same too. It would be less awkward, she figured, if they both felt the same. Wiping her mouth with the back of her sleeve, she stepped back into the room - the sound of people fucking instantly filling her ears.

Sam, Emma and Nick were standing against the wall. All of them were watching the couples going at it in the centre of the room; limbs everywhere as couples had becomes threesomes and - in some cases - more-somes.

Karen walked over to them with an air of confidence. One, she realised, which had been missing for far too long now.

Nick was the first to notice her. He smiled broadly.

"Hi," he said, extending his hand.

Karen giggled. It was funny shaking his hand considering - moments earlier - she had had his penis shooting directly into her mouth. The taste of his cum still lingering in her mouth. "Hello." She followed her greeting up with, "How are you doing?" It was a stupid question. Obviously he was doing well. She giggled again, "I'm sorry - stupid question. Ignore it."

He laughed as well, almost as though he were embarrassed, "I'm fine. Thank you." He hesitated a moment before, "And you?"

"I'm good. Pretty full!" she laughed.

He laughed too even though - going by his face - he didn't really see the need to. Emma and Sam stopped watching the group fuck a few feet away and turned to Karen.

"We thought we'd lost you!" Emma said.

"What? No. I was just," her face flushed again, "sorting myself out. Was feeling pretty hot after all this!"

Emma looked at her shocked. Here was a woman who had been accused of not being adventurous, slightly over a week ago, now telling them all she had just masturbated. How times had changed.

"I don't think I can keep Sam back for much longer," Emma laughed, "so we're going to leave you two to it, okay?"

"I think we'll be okay," Karen said. Much to her own surprise, she put her arm around Nick's waist. He didn't seem to mind, grinning like an idiot, he put his arm around her too. Karen smiled. Not only did he have a handsome cock but he was looking pretty damned good himself; dressed in a sleeveless latex shirt that clung to his muscles - and showed off an obvious six-pack hidden underneath - latex trousers that were tight at the thighs but flared at the ankles, and black DM boots. It was hard to tell in this light but Karen could have sworn he was wearing black eyeliner too.

"Check you out!" Emma was pleasantly surprised. She addressed Nick, "You wouldn't believe how shy she was about coming here and now look at her!"

"I am!" Nick quickly added, his eyes fixed on Karen and a broad grin still on his face.

"She's like a club regular!" Emma continued. She turned to Karen, "Okay the room is just through there at the back."

Karen giggled, "I know. That's where we were."

Emma frowned, "Who?"

Now Karen was frowning, "Me and Nick."

And Nick was frowning.

Karen noticed everyone's look and felt her face redden once more.

"What is it?" she asked.

"Who were you in the room with?" Emma asked, slightly concerned.

"Nick..."

"I think I'd remember that," Nick pulled away from Karen and looked at her, confused as to what the hell was going on. He wasn't the only one who was confused. They all were now. Emma and Nick because they'd been standing there - along with Sam who was still transfixed by the fucking on the beds - and Karen because she'd not long since swallowed someone's sperm.

Karen suddenly laughed, "Very good, you got me. Idiots, the pair of you."

"Karen - we've been here the whole time. We were looking for you, couldn't find you and thought you'd got cold feet... I sent you a text..."

"You know I left my phone at home."

"I told you to wait in here so you could at least know you were going into the room with the right partner..."

Karen repeated herself, "I told you I left my phone at home! Who the hell was in the other room then if it weren't Nick?"

"Karen? What are you doing here?" a voice came from behind her. Karen froze immediately. She hadn't heard it for a while but she recognised it immediately. Emma recognised them too - her eyes wide with disbelief. Of all the people to bump into and of all the places to do so. "Didn't know you came here too! Well, this isn't at all awkward," the man laughed.

Karen turned round and faced her younger brother. It wasn't just her face that was burning up, it was her whole body. The room so hot it felt as though the whole place should be on fire with flames licking the walls and pealing the skin from bodies as they writhed around fingering, licking, fucking, one another.

Karen stumbled over her words, "What are you doing here?" she asked.

Her brother smiled and pointed back towards the room at the rear, "I've just been in there!" he said. He was grinning from ear to ear, "Bit disappointed the chick who was in there disappeared so fast. Was hoping to at least get her number. She could suck a golf ball through a hose-pipe," he laughed. "Honestly... I think that was the fastest I've ever cum!"

No one was saying anything. They were just staring at her brother, mouths slightly agape and eyes wide. Karen was pale as a sickly green hue crept over her skin.

"You can't tell me that shocked you!" Her brother continued oblivious to what was going on, "I've caught you in the couples room - all four of you - clearly about to start fucking..." He suddenly looked at Nick and realised it wasn't Karen's husband. He looked back to Karen with an even more surprised look on his face, "Don't worry," he said with a wink, "your secret is safe... Anyway, if you don't mind... I need to get out of here before you start. The last thing I need to see is my sister's cunt!" He laughed. "Have a good evening!" And then he whispered to Karen, "Just remember to play safe. Chick in there ripped the rubber off... I could have pulled away but - fuck - felt so good... One thing getting a blow job through. Quite another having them fuck you. A lot easier catching stuff when penetration is involved, you know?" He laughed again, "Hey - least we'll have something to talk about come Christmas." He winked at Karen, "Catch you later!" And - with that, and without waiting for a goodbye from his clearly distracted sister and her equally distracted friends, he left the room.

The sound of couples fucking and having a good time did not drown out the sound of Karen retching.

THE END

HAIR OF THE DOG

1.

Regular as clockwork, Sean woke with a stomach ache: A harsh kicking on the inside of his belly as his intestines pulled and twisted within. He sat up in his bed and put pressure against his gut, pressing two hands there hard, wincing in pain. His partner - long gone - used to laugh at him when he got like this.

'Now you know how women feel!' she'd say, rather unhelpfully.

'Fuck you!' he'd always reply. And then - more or less in the same breath - he'd ask her to fetch him some laxatives. Kill the pain by clearing the system out, the only cure he knew to work when this hit home. Neck the pills, shit it out. Quick.

'Get them yourself!' she'd hiss - annoyed at being told to fuck off even though - deep down - she understood why he had snapped. He wasn't angry at her, he was just in pain. Even so, unless he said sorry, she wouldn't do anything for him. He needed to learn that you couldn't take your anger, or pain, out on other people. Especially people you were supposed to love. You needed to show respect. He had never apologised.

Another pang of pain thumped his insides causing him to bend further forward in his bed. A hard hit as though someone had punched him.

'Fuck!' he screamed out loud as the pain snapped him from the old memories of past unpleasant conversations with his ex.

Burning up - sweat dripping from his forehead - he flung his duvet away from him, exposing his body to the cold morning air. His gut visibly spasmed as yet another wave of intense pain hit hard. *God damn it.* He refused to shout out again.

He wouldn't give the pain the satisfaction of making him scream out for a second time. *The pain?* It was getting worse. Definitely more frequent with each passing second - not that Sean minded. The pain being more frequent just meant that *it* was coming, and that was good. The sooner *it* came, the sooner he'd be back to feeling himself again. Well, until next month that was when he would have to suffer it all over again. Still - what had he expected? You have a heavy night, you party hard for the evening… There has to be some consequences. That was the way life worked: Something good happens to you and it gets balanced out by something bad. That's life, pussy-cat.

Unsteady on his feet, Sean staggered through to the ensuite bathroom, ever thankful that he didn't have far to go. Not like the house he had shared with *her* just over a year ago. That place hadn't had an ensuite so he used to have to leave the bedroom, stumble his way down the hallway towards the bathroom. And it was guaranteed that she would always try and get there before him.

'Just a quick wee! You're going to be in there for ages!' She had had a point. When his stomach was this bad, he did end up sitting on the pan for longer than necessary. Not through choice but through necessity. He'd be there grunting and pushing and straining. This house was definitely better and for not the one "bathroom" reason but another reason too: *She* wasn't living there. It was just him. He could spend as long as he wanted in the bathroom and there was no one to hurry him up or call him "selfish" for taking so long. *Selfish?* Stupid bitch. *He didn't have a choice!* Although, he pointed this little fact out once - that it wasn't his fault. She had no sympathy and coldly replied with, 'Well you shouldn't have gone out last night then. You know I don't like it. And *you* know you can't handle it!'

Before sitting on the cold toilet seat, he pulled his shorts down and let out another groan of pain as he took yet another kick to the guts. It didn't matter how often he went through this, it never got any easier or more bearable. Was it worth it though? A question he often asked himself as his body worked the pain from his system. At this stage - getting comfortable on the toilet seat - it was hard to say. Thinking back to the previous night he was left with many a blackspot in his memories. *Come on, man, think... Think... Try and recall some fun to make all of this discomfort seem worthwhile. Let's see...*

The moon had been full. The air crisp. A pleasant evening. No other clear memories though. In fact there was nothing of his evening etched into his mind ready for playback. It was all a complete blank. The last memory he had from yesterday - perfectly crystal clear - was sitting in the pub garden, a pint of bitter in hand, watching the sun go down. He sighed. A rare moment of peace and tranquility in his over-complicated life. Another sigh. *Only yourself to blame...*

3

Memories. The memories would come throughout the month just as they always ,
had. There would be no warnings, there would be no rhyme and there would be no
reason as to how they came to him. They would just randomly pop back to him.
Sometimes they caused him to chuckle, occasionally they shocked him and -
periodically - they made him gag. *Wild times!*

An ache spasmed his stomach and his asshole twitched in preparation - an act
which reminded him that he was missing an important ingredient which made this
unpleasant experience run a little smoother… So to speak.

Sean reached across to the sink without getting up from the toilet. Next to the
cold water tap - where it always was - was a half-empty bottle of baby-oil. With the
thumb of his left hand he flicked the lid open. Holding his right hand open, he
squirted a healthy dose of oil into his palm. When he'd poured enough, he pushed
the lid down with the same thumb he had used to open the bottle. Then, without a
care, he dropped the bottle on the tiled floor.

Carefully he reached down, with his oiled hand, between his legs and up to
his arse crack. He rubbed the oil into his crack before using two fingers to ensure
most of the liquid was quickly mopped up and re-directed to his ring-piece.

'It's for the best,' he mumbled to himself, an excuse for what he was about to
do. Closing his eyes - off to a happy place - he pushed two fingers up inside his
anal passage to ensure the path was slippery for what it was about to push out.
When knuckle-deep, he felt something push back and shuddered. 'Fuck sake.'

Sean tore a sheet of toilet paper from the roll hanging on the holder and wiped his fingers clean. It's for moments like this he had a whole range of soap dispensers on a shelf above the sink, and just under the bathroom mirror. Various flavours and scents to hide the stink of filth from his violated fingers. He dropped the dirty sheet between his legs - and into the bowl - and sat there a moment readying to brace himself for what was to come. And it was coming. The pain had moved from his stomach to his lower back. It was definitely coming. *Regular clockwork. Tick, tock, tick, tock, tick...*

4

Sean suddenly winced and sat up straight. This burst of pain was more urgent than the last. His back ached, his stomach did too and - now - his ring was starting to sting as it began stretching around the cause of all of his discomfort. He scrunched his eyes together and pushed as hard as he could. *Just get it out. Get. It. Out.* Holding the sides of the toilet seat, he screamed out as he pushed as hard as he could. All the time he did so - as he did every month - he couldn't help but think of Elvis Presley. The King. A man who supposedly died on the toilet... There was more to it than that - there was always more to it - but Sean's mind didn't look at the details surrounding the death. It got stuck on the basic fact, the man died whilst sitting on the crapper and straining. Was this the fate that was in store for Sean too? A scary thought which caused him to take a break from straining - a little breather to catch his breath. Another thought which often popped into his head - at this the most unfortunate time - was one of rectal prolapsing.

A rectal prolapse happens when the rectum loses its normal attachments within the body. When this occurs it "telescopes" out through the anus or - to put it more simply - makes everything appear to turn inside out. It sounds horrific and is known to be uncomfortable *but* it is not a medical emergency. It was - however - pretty damned embarrassing, Sean thought, and the last thing he wanted happening to him. Even with the worry of straining so hard a blood vessel in his head burst, or his heart gave out, or even his rectum prolapsing - Sean took another deep breath and strained once more. After all, what choice did he have? He couldn't leave it up there without causing considerable discomfort and he sure as hellfire didn't want to go to the Accident and Emergency Department asking for medical assistance. *Jesus. Imagine the questions that would be asked.* No. He had no choice but to... *Push. PUSH! PUSH!*

Sean screamed again as he felt it slowly start to push through his ring-piece, stretching it wider the further it came out. He tried to ignore the pain - both from his ripping asshole and the pounding in his head from the pressure of the strain. He was so close. It was coming. The baby-oil lubricant was helping, as was his other friend in this situation - *gravity*. This is it. He was so close and then - for another month - it would be over and... SPLASH. Touchdown as it dropped from his arse and hit the water, causing a splash back to dampen his arse cheeks. *Nice.* But... It was over. His whole body relaxed and he let out a long suffering sigh. There might be more to come but that was definitely the worst of it. The stomach ache had passed and he felt as though he were near enough empty. Hell, it even felt as though it had been one of those pleasurable one-wipes: a shit so pure and clean that, actually, you don't require *any* wiping as not a trace has been left within you yet you still give it a courtesy wipe to be sure.

Sean tore a sheet of paper from the toilet-roll and reached down and behind him with it. Carefully - what with his asshole still sensitive from the over-stretching - he gave it a wipe. Then - as he often did - he pulled it back out from between his legs and gave the sheet a casual glance. No brown, just a light red. Light red was fine. Yes it was blood but it was only because something had ripped inside. Nothing major. Had it been major the blood would have been dark red. Light red was quite common after you'd had a hard stool. He scrunched the paper up by clenching his fist and got up from the toilet bowl. He turned to drop the paper down the toilet pan and froze when he saw what he'd just shit out. There, in the water slowly sinking to the bottom of the U-Bend, was a half-chewed hand.

Human.

The first memory flooded back to him.

5

'I hope you're going to pay for that!' The landlord of the pub shouted from the pub's doorway. He'd come out to clean away the glasses, left there by customers who'd either gotten chilly and gone in or gone home to be with their families as often the case at this time of the month. *Go home, lock the door, close the curtains and pray to God you wake up in the morning.* He was referring to the glass Sean had smashed, having accidentally knocked it from the table onto the ground. It was an accident, not done on purpose yet the landlord didn't seem to care and nor did he care that Sean appeared to be in considerable pain. 'I'm fed up with you lot coming here and smashing glasses, leaving me to clear the mess up. It's downright rude and uncalled for,' the landlord continued as he started clearing away glasses that *hadn't* been broken.

The sun had set and the moon had started its ascent into the twilight sky. Large and full, a spectacular sight as it appeared closer to the earth than it did on other nights - not that most people stood around admiring its beauty at *this* time of the month. Hell, even the landlord hadn't paid it any attention. He knew it was there and he knew he had to be quick with collecting the empties. There had been the usual warning on the News stations reminding people of the full moon and the landlord knew he had to get indoors and barricade himself and those who wanted to remain in for the night, drinking into the early hours with the fire roaring and the music playing. A night shared with mainly the older generation or those who felt their fellow patrons more family than their *actual* family.

The landlord finally noticed Sean as he dropped to the ground on all fours. In the dim light he could see the customer's skin was shimmering in the low-light as sweat dripped from his every pore. He didn't approach him though. He just stood there a moment, unsure of what to do. Was he supposed to just drop the glasses and run indoors, locking the door behind him, or was he to be the hero of the story and grab the double-barrelled shotgun from over the bar… End the town's nightmare once and for all and - no doubt - receive the Keys to the City for his heroic actions. Maybe even just say, 'Fuck 'em!' and run from the area and just keep on running until the sun rose up, bringing along the warmth, and safety, of a new day? Three possible options firing through his brain right there and then in a split second and yet - instead of acting upon any of them - he found himself calling out to Sean, 'Are you okay?'

Sean was on the grass now, writhing around in pain with his eyes screwed up shut. When he next opened them - at the sound of the landlord's relatively simple, yet pointless, question - they had a yellow hue to them. No longer were they the eyes of a man but something else entirely. The human scream of pain and despair turned into a lowly growl of an animal - a growl the town had heard time and time again across the years… Always at the same time of the month. The shocked landlord stepped back in terror as he dropped the glasses which he had just finished carefully stacking together. More than half of them smashed sending shards of glass across the ground.

'Please… Don't do this…' The landlord stuttered like an idiot. His feet glued to the ground in fear. A damp patch spreading at the front of his trousers. Warm urine down the leg. 'Please stop…'

More transformations. Skin was covered in a slowly thickening coat of coarse fur. Bones were cracking and distorting changing from human shape, snapping to a more canine-like appearance. No trace of human in the sounds being emitted from the throat. Growls - both of pain and hunger with the latter outweighing the first.

6

The yellow, harsh eyes turned to the frozen landlord and fixed on him. The beast's lips curled at the side showing the razor sharp teeth. Another growl. The landlord still didn't move. A thought, in his head, that he can't be seen if he doesn't move. It's like that scene in *Jurassic Park* - if only the lawyer had just stood still he would have survived. The landlord can survive this. He just needs to stand still… *He wouldn't be tomorrow's headlines.* He'll come to work, he'll laugh about what had happened, when recounting the story he'd ignore the fact he had pissed himself. The beast would charge him, he'd smack it in the face - maybe poke it in the eyes in the same way you'd save yourself from a shark attack? Was that a thing? Did it even…?

The beast - still on all fours - turned to the landlord. No trace of humanity there now, not in appearance nor the in the eyes. *Those eyes still fixed on the "food".*

The landlord was still thinking about shark attacks. Did it work when you poked them in the eye? How do you even poke a shark's eye when you're subjected to a frenzied attack? How…?

The beast pushed itself up so that it was on two legs now. A final few cracks in the bones as they adjusted at last. The moon was high in the sky now. Bright and illuminating the world below… The monster below. The moon's slave. Tilting his head back and looking up to the sky, the beast let out of a mighty howl which echoed across the pub gardens.

'Gerry, hurry up we heard…' One of the bar-staff had come out to find out where the landlord had got to. He never usually took this long collecting glasses especially when it hadn't even been *that* busy. Not compared to the proper summer nights when the whole garden would have been heaving. The girl - early twenties - saw the beast at the far end of the garden. It was the first time she had seen it. She'd heard the stories - some true, some fake - but she'd never seen it with her own eyes. When the howl finished, it fixed its eyes back to the landlord. The bar-staff screamed and disappeared back into the pub, slamming the door behind her. The sound of bolts and locks clicking across - much to the landlord's horror who'd suddenly snapped back to reality with a bump. He turned and ran towards the door, knocking on it and calling through.

'Open the door! Open the fucking door!'

The beast snarled. It liked it when they ran. It made more of a sport of it. And - it knew - the landlord was about to run. As soon as he realised his staff weren't going to risk their lives by opening the door - he would run. And when he did... The game was on. Another low growl.

'Open the...' The landlord realised they weren't opening anything. He was locked out and... *It was watching him, it had him in his sight.* He screamed through the door, 'Fuck you then! Fuck you, you cunts! You fucking cunts!' He kicked the door out of frustration and then started to run. Nothing chased him, not that he stopped running. The beast was just watching. A head start. A challenge. Sporting.

A snarl.

7

The chewed hand hit the bottom of the U-Bend. There was no way that was being flushed, not without flooding the bathroom and breaking the plumbing. With his eyes shut, Sean reached down and fished the hand out. Pappy skin, bits of blood, bits of shit. This was the part of the whole process Sean *hated*. Today was worse, though. That was his local. After a stressful day at work, he'd go there and he'd sink a few. Hell, he even liked drinking there after the full moon had gone. A few drinks to make himself feel a little better - the transformation process did take it out of him after all. The landlord was a friendly guy, most of the time. Yes, he got shitty if people were rowdy but if you treated him, his staff and his establishment with respect then he *was* a nice bloke. Emphasis on was.

Next to the toilet was a small cylinder bin with a foot pedal which opened the lid. Sean pressed his foot down on the pedal and - hey presto, just as planned - the lid opened. He dropped the hand into the bin, released his foot and watched as the lid slammed shut. He'd take it to the garden later and bury it. *Another bit to bury* and then - when that was done... He sighed... He'd start to look for a new local.

Damn it, you don't shit in your own back garden. Why couldn't the beast get this in its head? He had eaten the landlord, he had eaten the ex-girlfriend which in itself had forced him to move house... Now he had to move locals! He walked over to the bathroom mirror and stared at his reflection. He looked good. He always looked good *after* a night out on the town with the beast. It was only during the month, leading to the full moon, that he started to look more and more tired as his body geared up for the impending transformation... Sean suddenly laughed, he couldn't be too mad at the beast within. Eating the ex was definitely a good move. Not only did he get away with it (no body, just reported her as missing) but he also got a new place when her insurance paid out. That was definitely a plus... The landlord though... Sean stopped laughing. He'll have a shower, he'll get dressed and then, when he was ready, he'd find a new local. He'd bury the hand later. Drink first. Operation clean-up second. His stomach rumbled. Maybe a sandwich too. He looked back down to the bin, *shame to waste the left-overs.*

The End.

TEETH

1

There are thirty-two teeth in the average human

which - not everyone gets. If you watch *Jeremy*

fact but it is true. The average healthy human m

of incisors, canines, premolars and then - at the back - molars. Just to

things though, Emma is an average human being but she doesn't have a full set of

teeth. She hasn't had them for some time thanks to a diet high in sugar and poor

hygiene with regards to brushing. That's not to say she didn't brush her teeth, it's

just that she didn't brush them *properly.*

Needless to say - the dentist wasn't her favourite place and yet that was

exactly where she found herself today. She was sitting in a busy waiting room

nervously trying to forget previous uncomfortable visits to the surgery. Trying and

failing. Sweat very visibly dripped from her forehead but no one said anything. No

one had a right to. After all, she wasn't the only one sitting there with a pale

complexion.

'Mr. Wright?' An olive-skinned dental nurse in a neat blue uniform poked her

head around the door of the dentist's office. She was looking around the waiting

patients, hoping to catch the eye of Mr. Wright - the man who was due in the chair

next. 'Mr. Wright?' the lady asked again as an elderly man stood up with shaking

legs.

Even though it wasn't her name, Emma's heart still skipped a beat. It was one

step closer to her own appointment - an appointment she already knew wouldn't be

a pleasant experience thanks to the toothache she'd had for the last week. A dull

throb which woke her one night and then kept her awake until morning. Within two

as no longer a dull throb but - instead - an intense ache that got worse
when she put pressure on it. Much worse.

The ticking clock, hanging on the wall, seemed to tick and tock louder -
drumming that her time was coming. *It'll be your turn soon. It'll be your turn and
he'll be stabbing you with sharp needles, he'll be drilling you. He'll be clamping
your tooth with those pliers. He'll be twisting and tugging and pulling and your
gum will be ripping with the nerves screaming. Tick, tock. Tick, tock...*

'Good morning,' the nurse greeted Mr. Wright as the old man reached her.
'You okay?'

'Very well, thank you.'

He stepped into the room and the door was closed behind him. Emma looked
down at the magazines on a small table in the centre of the room. Chipped paint
and ugly, out of place in a waiting area that had only recently been refurbished.
The magazines were out-dated too. One of them, she noticed, was over six months
old. It pissed Emma off, not because she liked reading but because it wouldn't kill
them to keep the magazines updated. It's not as though dentist appointments were
cheap and they couldn't afford new literature. They were just lazy. Even so, she
picked a magazine up and started thumbing through the well-read pages. Adverts,
stories of marital betrayal, horoscopes, more adverts… Emma sighed and tossed
the magazine back down on the table.

The door to the surgery opened and old Mr. Wright came back out smiling. He
didn't close the door behind him as he approached the reception desk where the
receptionist greeted him with a smile.

'That was quick.'

'Perks of being old. Not many teeth for him to check.'

The receptionist laughed.

'Would you like to book another appointment?'

'Yes please.'

'For six months time I take it?'

'Indeed.'

Emma watched, enviously, as the receptionist checked her system for the next available date.

'April 16th?'

'Perks of being retired. I'm pretty much free all of the time.'

'What time would you prefer?'

'Ooh, how about morning? Get it out of the way so I can enjoy the rest of my day.'

'Sounds like a good plan.' The receptionist looked back down to her diary. 'We have eight forty-five?'

'Perfect.'

The middle-aged woman scribbled down the date on a *reminder* card. She handed it to Mr. Wright and said, 'So that's just thirty-five pounds to pay for today's check-up then.'

Mr. Wright reached into the back pocket of his trousers and removed his tatty, brown leather wallet. Opening it up, he took out his credit card and slid it into the front of the card machine resting on the reception counter. 'You would think I would get discount considering there is less teeth to check.' It was a comment meant in jest but - as soon as he said it - he started to wonder whether he actually *should* get discount. After all, there was less work in his mouth than a younger person with all their teeth. Although, he quickly argued in the dentist's defence, less teeth didn't mean less work. Some people only have a few pegs in their stinking mouths and even those are rotting and needing attention.

'Doesn't work like that I'm afraid,' the receptionist said, thinking he was being serious.

'I know, I know.' Mr. Wright smiled at her as he entered his pin into the card machine. Seconds later, the card was authorised and the receipt printed off. He removed the card and slotted it back into his wallet, along with the appointment card for six months time. 'Well, I'll see you in six months then!'

'See you then,' the receptionist said with a smile. 'Have a good day…' And, with that, Mr. Wright turned and walked from the surgery to enjoy whatever else he had planned for his day.

Lucky bastard, Emma thought.

Tick, tock, tick, tock, tick, tock…

'Emma Keane?' The dentist's assistant called out from the doorway. Emma's heart skipped a beat.

Shit.

2

Emma walked into the room, nervously. The assistant had already walked back to the other side of the room and started going through various instruments making sure everything was present and okay.

'Hello, Emma.' The dentist smiled. His voice sounded pleasant enough. He was good looking with his dark hair, dark eyes, athletic looking body under his scrubs but... Emma remembered the first time she had seen him. She felt her face flush. He was exactly her type of man looks-wise, not that she had ever told him that. He was, after all, a dentist and that meant he was a sadist. So, yes, he looked the part of perfect boyfriend but behind that crocodile smile, there was nothing but pain and misery. 'How have you been?' he asked. He wasn't asking about her as a person. He was asking after her teeth. How had *they* been. This was something Emma learned the hard way after going into great detail about how she was doing when they had first met. Throughout her whole spiel he just looked at her, smiling. When she was done - he simply said, 'Any problems with your teeth or gums?' Emma didn't understand why he asked this time. He knew there was a problem. It was the reason why she had phoned up and made the appointment.

Emma cut the pleasantries and got down to business. 'It's the tooth at the back.' She pressed her finger up against her cheek and flinched when she inadvertently pressed too hard, setting the tooth off again. 'Been hurting for a week now and gets worse if I bite down on it...'

'Okay well, if you'd like to take a seat we'll have a look and see what is going on back there. Any issues apart from that?'

'No.' Emma sat on the dentist chair and tried to make herself as comfortable as possible. (So not very comfortable at all). The dental nurse laid a plastic bib over Emma's chest.

'If you could just put these on.' The nurse handed her a pair of plastic spectacles. Emma put them on, even though she hated wearing them. She just felt stupid in them. Self-conscious at the thought of the dentist and his assistant laughing at how ridiculous she looked.

By the time the dentist came back into view, he was wearing a mask that covered his nose and mouth. He reached to the tray of instruments beside him. Emma closed her eyes. She didn't need to see what he was doing and what he was holding. It didn't help with her nerves. It made them worse.

'Okay, open wide.'

Emma opened her mouth.

'Let's take a look...'

With her hands shaking, Emma gripped the sides of the chair and squeezed as hard as she could. *It's thirty minutes. Thirty minutes of unpleasantness and then it is done. Just... Be brave...* But it wasn't thirty minutes of pain and unpleasantness. Sure, this appointment might last that and this toothache would then be gone but there'd be something else. There'd be another filling required, or another de-scaling with the hygienist - along with a mouthful of blood - and then there'd be something else and something else after that and... Emma flinched as the dentist pressed against the bad tooth. He muttered something to the nurse.

'Okay.' He pulled away from Emma. Emma opened her eyes. 'I'd say you have an abscess. We'll do an X-Ray to confirm but - moving forward - we have two options. The first being that we can pull the tooth right out. The second is a root canal…'

'No!' Emma cut him off. 'No root canal.' Her mind flooded with memories of her last dentist and the root canal treatment they had performed on her. Four painful injections supposedly used to numb all pain and yet she had felt everything. And then there was the bleach. They had put a protective rubber shield in her mouth which had a tiny hole in it. It was placed over the tooth being worked on, with only that poking through the hole. The point of the shield was to protect the rest of the mouth as they washed the recently-drilled root out with bleach, sprayed by the dental nurse. The shield didn't work and the bleach leaked through to the back of Emma's throat. She didn't make a fuss. She laid there, waiting for them to finish with her eyes shut; screwed-up tightly. But the bleach burned, stuck at the back of her throat because she refused to swallow. Boy did it burn. And the burns? They blistered. 'Take the tooth out,' Emma said.

'It's your choice but you're already missing two teeth back there. It might be better if we try and save…'

'I want it out. Can you take it out now?'

'I'm afraid we don't have the time to perform an extraction now. This was just an appointment to assess your tooth, to see where we go from here. What we can do is drill down into it for you in order to let it drain. It will relieve some of the pressure from the infection and the pain - then - we can schedule you in for tomorrow?' He continued, 'And I can prescribe you some pain-relief in the meantime too. Something stronger than what you can get over the counter.' Emma wasn't really listening to him. Her mind was stuck on Mr. Wright - the old man from earlier. Not him as a person but more what he had said when he left the dentist's room. The conversation between the receptionist and Mr. Wright… She said he had been quick. He replied it was a perk of being old - there weren't many teeth to check. Better than that - he didn't need to go back to the dentist for six months!

'Take them all out.' Emma sat up excitedly. The dentist looked at her, confusion etched on his face. Emma repeated herself so there was no misunderstand, 'I want you to remove *all* of my teeth.'

'All of them? Are you having problems with them?'

'No but… Every time I see you I need a filling or something else. If I have them removed, it will save hassle and pain in the future. One painful day and then it will be over with. I'll get to see you on a six monthly basis like the old man who was just in here…' She carried on, excited at the prospect of doing things on her terms now, 'And there's these implants I was reading about. Apparently they just screw into sockets in the gums?'

'Well yes but that is a very expensive procedure…' Dental implants are created by placing small posts - made of titanium - directly into the bone socket of the missing teeth. As the jawbone heals, it grows around the implanted post which - in turn - anchors it securely in position. It's not a pleasant experience and can take between six and twelve weeks to heal completely. Once the implant has bonded to the jawbone, another small post - an abutment - is attached to the post. This is what holds the new tooth. With regards to the teeth themselves, they're created using an impression of your teeth. The dentist creates a model of your bite and - hey presto - a new tooth (a crown) is created. This is then attached to the abutment. Once the missing teeth are replaced, the dentist would then colour them so they look more natural and in line with your other teeth. When researching dental implants (purely by accident) Emma thought this bit to be the weird step. She had thought, had she gone through with the operation herself, that she would want brilliant white teeth. A bit like Simon Cowell's almost *too perfect* teeth. 'And you already have teeth which would also require removal which would add to the cost. A basic extraction, at the moment, is approximately fifty pounds under the National Health…'

'I don't care. I want dental implants.'

'We could look at getting implants for the teeth you're missing or - of course - there is the option of false teeth. We could bridge between…'

'No. That would defeat the purpose. I would still have teeth which would require looking after and…' Emma found herself getting irritated. 'I do all I can for my teeth. I brush twice a day, I floss, I mouthwash and yet I still have issues. I just want them taken out.'

'These would still…'

'Look it doesn't matter what you say. They're my teeth. I want them out.'

'It's painful…'

'I would get it done and that would be it, though. I wouldn't need to come back other than for check ups and if there was a problem you could just unscrew the tooth and…'

'It doesn't really work like that. And then of course there is the fact they would still need to be looked after. They can still…'

'They would be better than my own teeth. Look, I am going to do this. If you don't want to do it there will be plenty more dentists who would be more than willing.'

The dentist shrugged. 'There will be forms to fill in. Waivers and such. But, before we do anything, we need to sort your infected tooth out to save you from being in pain.'

'You can schedule me in to do all of them at once. I just want it over and done with…'

'Your gums will need to heal over before we can…'

'I don't care. I just want it over and done with.'

The dentist stopped talking. He knew it was pointless. Emma had made her mind up and - at the end of the day - they *were* her teeth.

'If you'd like to lay back down, we'll see about relieving some of that pain…'

Emma laid back down and - for the second time - closed her eyes.

3

Emma was sitting in the dentist's leather chair. She was tonguing the hole drilled in her rotten tooth during the previous appointment. That had been a week ago. A week of trying to keep the damned hole clean and free from food debris whilst she waited for today to come round. Her last painful appointment. Both upper and lower gums were completely numb after a series of injections. The dentist had taken an impression of her teeth, done various X-Rays and discussed the implications of what they were going to do today. Implications Emma didn't really listen to. The dentist had told her there was a chance her remaining teeth might have been perfect for the rest of her life, not needing any work to be done but… Emma knew better. Sooner or later, they'd need something done to them. Even if it was just a filling. That's where it always started. A filling here, then a bigger filling and then… Root canal treatment.

'Everything should be feeling pretty numb right about now,' the dentist said.

Emma nodded. The dentist lifted a dental elevator from a tray his nurse had set up prior to the appointment's start time. The dental elevator was a small tool which looked a little like a screw driver. The design was formed in such a way it allowed the tool to be wedged into the ligament space between the tooth and its surrounding bone. As the elevator is forced in and twisted around in this space, the tooth is pressed and rocked against the bone. An act which helps to expand the socket and separate tooth from its ligament. A simple extraction on a tooth clearly visible. The best place to start, the dentist figured. Especially with a patient this nervous.

Using a narrow elevator, he started to wedge it between tooth and gum. He hoped that the first tooth would be an easy one. One to set the tone for the rest of the extractions. A little wiggling, a satisfying crack and out it would pop. Worst case - he'd have to use the forceps to finish the job. Grab them from the top, pull from side to side and... Pop.

'Then let's get started. If you feel any pain - put your hand up right away and I'll stop. Okay?'

Emma nodded again. She closed her eyes and prepared herself. The dentist forced the elevator between tooth and gum. Emma's hands clenched either side of the chair... *It's one more appointment of pain, followed by an operation to get the implants put in and then that's it. Six month check-ups here on in and nothing else. No more injections. No more pain. No more needles. No more drilling.... Just get through today.* She scrunched her eyes tighter together as she felt the full weight of the dentist press down upon the tooth. He pushed one way. He pulled another way. He twisted. He pulled again. Pushed. Twisted the opposite direction. Pulled. Pulled. Twisted. Pushed. Pulled. CRACK. Relief. Despite the numbness, she felt the tooth slowly slide from the bone as the dentist pulled tooth and root out in one satisfying movement. *One down.* The tooth made a soft thud as the dentist dropped it onto the tray at his side. The assistant used the suction machine to remove some of the fresh blood filling the new hole and spilling over into Emma's mouth.

'How are you feeling?' the dentist asked Emma. She answered by raising her right thumb. *"A-Ok".* He'd pulled a lot of teeth in his time but this was a first; pulling all the teeth from someone in one go. Still - it was her choice. He had told her that they wouldn't be able to do anything with regards to the implants for about a month, give or take, so that her gums had a chance to heal from the bruising they'd experience from today's trauma. She had agreed. He had told her she was choosing to rip out some perfectly healthy teeth (healthy for now, at least) and - again - she had agreed. He had told her the costs of the implants and she had said she'd find the money come rain or shine so… It was all down to her. As a professional, he knew he had done all he could to put her off from doing this. *This was her choice.* He shrugged. No sense wasting time wondering if he was doing the right thing. Just get on with it. Carefully he pushed the elevator down between tooth and gum - right down as far as it needed to go. For the second time he applied all of his weight, pulling down on it and pushing back again, rocking the tooth from the bone. With each movement he made, Emma worked her head in the opposite direction in an effort to help loosen the tooth. Just like the first one, this cracked away with minimal fuss too. *Damn.* The dentist pulled the broken tooth from Emma's mouth and dropped it onto the tray. Setting aside the elevator he lifted one of the pairs of forceps the assistant had prepared; the one he figured best fit for the tooth. He grasped the remaining stump of the tooth just beneath what remained of the crown and above the root section and started wiggling it from side to side. With each wiggle, a little rotating of his wrist - twisting it in its socket. The twisting helped as it gradually ripped and tore the tooth away from the ligament that bound it in its place. More pressure. It wouldn't be long now. The socket was already expanding. Tear the ligament a little more and - out it would pop. *CRACK.* Emma squirmed in the seat as the dentist disposed of the broken fragment. Two down. More blood sucked up by the dental nurse who worked carefully to avoid catching Emma's tongue. The dentist had suggested two appointments at least to get this done but she had insisted on the one. *Brave woman.* Onto the third…

4.

Four days since the appointment and Emma's mouth was still sore. She had
expected that to be the case but - even so - she had hoped there would be some
times at least when it wouldn't hurt quite as much. Every couple of hours she
swilled warm salt water around her mouth. An act which stung like a son of a bitch
but would apparently help with the healing process. Still, the sting took away from
her pounding headache. A headache caused by sleepless nights thanks to the pain
in her mouth.

Standing in the kitchen, Emma turned the gas hob off. The soup was bubbling
away nicely, ready to eat. Four days of pain and four days of tomato-flavoured
soup. The only flavour she could stomach. Lifting the saucepan by the handle, she
poured the steaming contents into a large bowl she'd set on a tray next to a spoon.
It was the middle of the night and she wasn't hungry but knew she had to eat as the
painkillers would be wearing off soon and she'd be ready for the next dosage. *Take
two pills on a full stomach.* She walked through to the living room. The television
was on, playing through some crappy soap about flying doctors. One channel had
this, one channel had a recording of a card game of all things, one channel had an
old black and white movie - something, she presumed, to be direct from the
Hammer archives... Nothing worth watching much to her frustration. Something
else to piss her off about not being able to sleep; nothing decent on the television to
help keep her entertained in the early hours. On more than one occasion she had
looked longingly at her phone and wished to phone a friend. She didn't have many
and those she did have wouldn't have been thankful for a call at this time of the

morning. Besides, she couldn't talk to them. They'd sense something was wrong and they'd want to come over and… She hadn't told anyone about her dentist appointment and didn't want them seeing her with no teeth. No teeth and all gums. She only wanted to see them again once she had a full set of pearly whites and… *God.* Not for the first time she realised just how long she had to wait before she could smile with a full set of perfect whites once more. Even when the gums healed, she couldn't afford the implants immediately. Her credit card had been maxed out on having the real teeth removed and she'd been signed off work for a month whilst her gums healed; something she had to beg the doctor to do.

Emma worked in retail. She knew she couldn't very well go into the shop with a mouth full of gum and gore. Not just because she needed time to heal and get the bleeding under control but because people wouldn't want to be served by her. She worked in fashion and this look was hardly fashionable. If anything, her being there would drive the customers away to the competition. When she broke down in front of the doctor, he signed her off with depression. As it often did, when Emma got thinking, her mind started wondering how she'd be able to pay for the implants. She had told the dentist it wouldn't be a problem when he came back with the high-end of the four figure bill. *She had savings.* The most she had in her savings account, meant for a girls' holiday next year, was a couple of hundred pounds. That wouldn't even pay for one tooth and - even if it did - she wouldn't have been able to afford the screw-socket for it to sit in. *Shit.*

Emma flicked the television channel up one. She already knew that there was nothing on but surely there must have been something on one of the many channels that could have distracted her better than flying doctors. The screen flickered. Motorway cops were in high pursuit of… The screen flickered. The news anchorman read from the autocue with a serious expression. There had been an uprising of… The screen flickered. An over-the-top gameshow host introduced another man looking for a date. Standing before the host and the contestant were a number of attractive women - all smiling their perfect smiles and… The screen flickered. An African family looked directly out of the screen with long faces. A narrator explained how far they had to travel for… The screen flickered. A stunningly attractive girl laid on a bed in nothing but skimpy lingerie. She had a phone pressed to her ear. A number - *her number* - scrolled across the bottom of the screen. With her spare hand, she twirled her long blonde hair around her finger, teasingly so. Emma didn't change the channel. This woman, whoever she was, had her attention and not for reasons which might have been obvious to late night lurkers looking through the window. She had her attention because she reminded Emma of adverts in magazines she'd seen over the years. Small box adverts on the back pages of pretty girls offering phone sex on premium rate numbers. *An easy way to make money.* For a moment, just a moment, there was no pain in her mouth.

*

Emma looked like a crazy lady. Her hair was a tangled mess. There were heavy bags under her eyes from the lack of sleep since the procedure. Her mouth… The fact she was wearing a dressing gown and slippers didn't help either, not that the shopkeeper said anything. Working through the night - alone - he knew better than to try and question someone or even laugh at them. For all he knew, they were addicted to drugs and ready to kick off at any given moment. It was definitely better to keep quiet! Besides, she was in slippers and her dressing gown. She was probably just a housewife who'd remembered she had no milk for the kids' morning breakfast. Milk and bread maybe. Could have just gone to make herself a cup of tea and realised the milk was off. Or she'd gone for a late snack and seen the bread was mouldy so she *had* to come out. Yes. That would be it That would make sense. She wasn't a crazy lady. She was a lady on a mission. A lady wanting to ensure her children had the best start for the day. They say, after all, that breakfast is the most important meal of the day.

'These please.' Emma put a collection of adult magazines down on the counter - much to the shock of the shopkeeper. Emma noticed the shocked look on the man's face. 'It's for the articles...'

'Uh huh.'

5

'Hey, baby…' A seductive, husky voice purred down the other end of the phone, breathing heavily as though in a high state of arousal. Emma didn't say anything. She just sat there, on her sofa, with her hand pressed against the mouth-piece so that she wouldn't be heard. 'What's your name?' the lady asked between soft moans. Emma didn't answer. 'Silent-type, huh? Shame… I'd love you to tell me what you're wearing right now. Hopefully nothing. Hopefully you're sitting there, naked, with your big, hard cock in your hands - slowly stroking it up and down as you think of me sitting here naked. Are you doing that? Are you touching yourself? Mmmm. I hope so. It makes me so wet to think of you doing that…' The phone went silent for a split second before the woman started moaning. 'Mmmmm. Do you know what I'm doing now?' Emma pictured the woman in her home, sitting up in bed having been disturbed from her sleep by Emma's call. She envisioned her messy hair, tired look and partner lying next to her - also having been disturbed - trying not to laugh at what she was doing. The woman continued with a sigh, 'I'm touching myself. Stroking my clit with my fingers. Are you touching yourself?' She moaned in pleasure again. 'Mmmmm. I'm so wet for you, baby. I wish you were here… I wish your cock was sliding in and out of my juicy cunt. Is that what you're picturing? My tight pussy wrapped around your hard cock…' Emma tried not to laugh and wondered how the Hell this woman wasn't in fits of giggles herself. It was the most ridiculous thing she'd ever heard but - that being said - it was also one of the easiest things too. Sit at home, wait for lonely perverts to phone up, pretend to get off whilst they wank themselves and get paid by the minute… All she needed to do was set up a premium rate number and get an advert in a magazine. Then it was just a case of waiting for the callers to phone in. The stranger sucked on her finger and moaned again. 'Mmmm. My juices taste so sweet. Imagine pushing your tongue into my cunt, soaking them…'

Emma cut her off and said, 'How do you set these numbers up?' The woman on the other end of the phone stopped acting. There was silence. Emma explained, 'I want to set one up too but don't know how to go about it.'

The woman stumbled over her words. 'Y-You want to set one of these numbers up?' She had been doing this job for a while. In fact - she owned 25% of the numbers on the page Emma had first discovered her on. All the adverts were of different women in different poses and offering a different style of phone sex. Call through for a dominant woman, a submissive woman, to eavesdrop on a woman masturbating… The more numbers on the phone - the more adverts - the more chance of someone calling her. It made for good business sense. All she had to do was remember which mobile was for which service - helped by the fact she labeled the phones with a coloured dot. Red was dominant. White was submissive. Yellow was for the people wanting to eavesdrop. She asked again, 'You want to set one of these numbers up?'

'Yes. I'm…' She stopped. The woman didn't need her life story. 'I was just wondering if you could tell me how you did it?' The woman didn't hang up - as you'd expect from most business owners in a similar position. When someone phones you up saying they want to set up a business in direct competition to you, it's the natural thing to do: Hang up. The woman was a business woman and she was a good one at that - hence the multiple adverts in the same magazine (and in other magazines too). She was also paid by the minute and the longer she could keep Emma on the phone, the more money she got. Yes, she was a good business woman.

'It's not that easy...' she said slowly.

'To do the job or set the line up?'

'There are five steps that you need to follow in order to set up a premium rate number and - I'll be honest - they're not especially easy. They can take time and they can be frustrating...' The woman's voice had changed from the seductive tones of a woman trying to get a man off and switched to something more *matter of fact*. 'It's not actually a quick way of making money, like people believe it is. And with lines like this? It's even harder thanks to the free pornography readily available online. The only good thing is at least with these services people get to talk to a real person which - obviously - they don't when watching pornographic clips.' She continued, 'Well - I say that is a good thing but most men get off through visual stimuli...' The woman continued to talk but Emma had stopped listening. Her enthusiasm had dwindled at the prospect of it taking time to set up and not being a quick way of making cash. She wanted new teeth as soon as she possibly could, not months down the line. She couldn't hide away for months and certainly couldn't stay away from work. The woman was still talking, 'It does tend to be older people calling me I have to say...' She laughed. 'That's good though because it takes them longer...' Her words were falling on deaf ears. Emma's eyes had been drawn to another advert in the back of the magazine. Sexual services were offered but not via a telephone service. This was more direct. This was more hands-on. Emma hung the phone up, cutting the lady off mid-sentence. Her mind was already exploring the many avenues of her next brainwave. *Easy money.*

6

It had been a month since the dentist appointment. The dentist smiled and said that Emma's gums had healed enough for her to be able to have the next operation - the putting in of the fixtures for her new teeth. He didn't discuss the financial side of things. He presumed she would have had the money ready considering this had been her idea in the first place and they'd already gone through the costings.

'Just book in with reception and we'll…'

'Not yet. I'm not ready yet.'

The dentist frowned. 'I'm sorry?'

'I'm not ready yet.'

He presumed she was just nervous about another procedure. 'It's a relatively straight forward…'

'I'm sorry to cut you off but I really need to go. Are we done?' Emma got up from the dentist chair and started putting her coat back on having taken it from the coat peg in the corner of the room where she'd previously hung it. The dentist was taken aback. 'I have another appointment.' She turned the conversation back to her mouth. 'But the gums are looking good? I mean, they're good?'

'Healed nicely. You used the salt water?'

Emma answered with a gummy smile. 'I did.' Emma took a scarf from her pocket and wrapped it around her face, hiding her mouth. She mumbled through the material, 'See you in six months?'

The dentist frowned, 'Six months? But don't you want to get…'

'That's great. Thank you!' Emma walked from the room, without letting the dentist finish what he was saying. She booked in to come back within six months and - with a skip in her step, along with a sense of urgency - she walked from the building towards the new BMW parked up in the car park. Emma climbed in and put the key in the ignition before leaning over to the glovebox. A press of the release button and it dropped open revealing two mobile phones. She took them both out and glanced at the screens. On one phone there were three missed calls and one message. The second phone just had a single text message: *free today?* She smiled behind the scarf and dropped the phones onto the passenger seat next to her. She'd listen to the message and reply to the text later. Right now, she needed to get back home. She started the car's two litre engine with ease, selected first gear and gently pulled away from the parking space. Pressing her foot down gently on the accelerator, she started to gather speed unaware that the dentist was peering through the blinds in his office. A look of confusion on his face. Fine, she might not have wanted the procedure to be done but - at the very least - she could have had some dentures ordered. Surely that had to be better than nothing? He stepped back from the window and the blinds swung shut. It was her choice. All of this - everything - was *her* choice.

Ten minutes later and Emma turned into the driveway of her home, not that it would be her home for much longer. She'd never liked it here and had recently given notice to move out somewhere a little nicer. Not just that - but she was moving to a bigger property too. Two bedrooms to four bedrooms. And a garage, something else she'd missed from this property but then, no surprise there given the amount of rent she paid in the current property. Could hardly expect luxury when she paid so little.

Emma climbed from her car and hurried up to - and through - the front door with handbag in one hand and mobile phones grasped in the other; one of which was ringing again. *They'll leave a message.* She pushed the door shut with a twerk of her arse before dropping her bag in the hallway. Quickly, she hurried up the stairs and into her bedroom. The curtains were closed, the bed was made, the Yankee candle was ready to be lit. Everything was ready. Everything - that is - other than her and she wouldn't take long. All she had to do was remove her dress which - she undid the zip at the back and wiggled from it - never took long. A quick glance in the mirror hanging on the wall opposite the bed. She looked good standing there in her lingerie and stockings, the scarf still wrapped around her neck and mouth. That - for this - she never took off. Not until it was time, for the simple fact, it wasn't attractive. It *felt* good for them but it didn't *look* good. She walked over to the bedside cabinet, in the corner of the room, and sprayed perfume into the air before stepping into the scented cloud. She'd done the same before she went to the dentist but it didn't hurt to freshen up a little, especially as she'd sweated whilst in the dentist's chair, even though she had no reason to. Anyway - just like that - she was ready. All she needed now was… There was a knock from downstairs. The front door. Her client. Bang on time.

*

His name was Luke, a young man in his mid-twenties - about ten years younger than Emma. He was standing, nervously, on her doorstep with a smile on his face intended to hide his obvious apprehension at his booking.

'Chantal?' he asked. A quiver in his voice.

'Please - come in.' Emma held the door open. Luke stepped in and Emma closed the door.

'I like your scarf,' he said - seemingly too nervous to mention the fact she was wearing nothing else but lingerie. He figured, if he mentioned the lingerie first… He'd come across as a pervert. But then… He had booked this woman for half an hour of… Doesn't that make him a pervert?

'Thank you.'

He reached into his pocket and pulled out some money. 'This is for you,' he said as he handed it to Emma. She took it from him. £100. *Another* £100. In the last three weeks she had paid off her credit card. She had even saved the money for the rest of the dental procedure - but she had also done some thinking. It really was easy money. Card paid off, dental procedure money saved, new car from BMW (on finance but, deposit paid). If she carried on like this, she could pay the car off within the year *and* go on holiday. Holiday? She smiled from behind the scarf. She couldn't remember the last time she had a holiday which involved a plane journey and - better yet - actual sunshine.

'Thank you.' She tucked the money into her bra for safe-keeping. 'Can I get you a drink?'

'I'm good, thank you.'

'Well then… If you'd like to follow me…' Emma walked slowly up the stairs, conscious of the fact Luke was close behind. She knew what she was doing; walking with an extra *wiggle* in her arse. Her client would be the same as all the others who had come before him and she *knew* his eyes would be fixed firmly on her G-string clad arse. He could look, but he couldn't have it. At the top of the stairs she turned into the bedroom and made her way to the bed. She turned and sat on the edge of it, her eyes fixed on her client. He hesitated in the doorway, clearly nervous of what was to follow. Emma patted the mattress next to where she was sitting. 'Come on then.'

'I'm sorry. I'm new to this. I mean - not *this* but…'

'Someone like me?'

Luke smiled. He was embarrassed. He went to say something but stuttered over his words and ended up forming none of the ones he intended.

'Relax. You're in good hands.' She patted the bed again. Luke smiled again and took a step closer, ready to sit with her. Emma stopped him, holding her hand up. 'You might want to lose the clothes first…'

Luke undid his belt and lowered both trousers and boxers. He kicked them out of the way and stood there, awkwardly, with his shirt and socks still on. His penis was embarrassingly flaccid. He looked down to it and then up to Emma, almost nervous of her reaction to such a sorry sight. *She was used to this, right? She'd seen it time and time before, yeah?*

'Relax…' Emma patted the bed. Luke walked over and sat beside her with his hands by his side. 'Trust me - you're in for a good time… You read the feedback from previous clients? The best, they said.'

'I know. It's just… Not sure what to expect…'

Emma slowly - seductively - removed her scarf. She put it around Luke's neck and smiled at him; a toothless, gummy smile. She told him, 'You're in for the softest, wettest oral pleasure of your life.' Slowly, surely, she moved down until he felt her breath against his flaccid cock. 'So just sit back and relax… Go with it…' And, with that, she wrapped her lips around his penis - her gums pressing down upon it. She started to suck. Luke flopped back against the firm mattress. As his penis started to harden, his eyes rolled to the back of his head. As Emma started to gather rhythm, keen to get it over with, she started imagining all she could do with the money. She already had the car - which would be paid off fast, she had the new clothes, she had the new home... Next up, she'd have a holiday. A nice holiday somewhere hot and exotic. She'd have it all and... Luke moaned out loud as he suddenly shot his hot load down the back of Emma's throat. She swallowed it down without a problem.... She'd have it all and then, *then*, she'd get her teeth fitted...

The End.

Note from the author:

Are you squeamish about dentists? I am. Once, I had excruciating toothache. My tooth right at the back of my mouth was throbbing like an absolute bastard. One thing made it feel better though and that was pressure. So I pushed on the side of the tooth and - for a moment - the pain was gone. So I kept pushing and kept pushing and kept and snap. The tooth actually cracked and was wobbling around. Not good but the pain was - at least - gone. So - next up - I went into the garage and dug out my old man's pliers. What happened next was, for me, a better alternative than going to the dentist. I opened my mouth, I put the pliers in, I gripped the tooth and I twisted and twisted until it pulled from my mouth. Or rather, I pulled some of it from my mouth. I left the root in. But still, the pain was gone so I ignored it. Over the coming months, the gum healed over the root and I forgot about it until I was - one day - brave enough to go for a real dentist appointment. It was during this appointment they did an X-Ray and saw the mess I had made. They advised that I needed the root out or else I could have real problems in the future… Well, okay, they know best. How did they get the root out? They cut into the gum with a scalpel and then ripped it out with more pliers. I bled for a day. The moral of this story, if you're taking your tooth out - get the root too!!!

<u>ELEVEN</u>

The following Short Story is only available in **The Black Room Manuscripts Volume 2**.
If you have not already purchased this title, please do give it a look on Amazon.
All proceeds from BRM2 go to **Alzheimer's Research UK**.

Eleven years old.

Tight little skirt. Grey. See-through white shirt with a white lace bra beneath, not that there was much to fill it. White cotton pop-socks up to her scrawny knees. Cotton underneath the skirt too? The man licked his lips. A tie tied loosely around her neck with the top button of the shirt undone. Mouse-blonde hair down to her shoulders. He wished it had been fashioned into pig-tails as opposed to hanging freely - as he'd requested in the chatroom. Fringe down her forehead, just above her eyes and covering her eyebrows. A smile.

That smile. The smile from the photo.

Pretty as a picture.

"You came," he smiled.

"You invited me," she walked in; school bag slung over her left shoulder.

Eleven years old with the confidence of a young woman.

The man watched her as she walked down the hallway towards his living room, his eyes fixed upon her tight rear-end for longer than necessarily decent. Another lick of his lips and a quick glance outside of his apartment - down either end of the corridor. No one out and about. No witnesses to his little visitor. He closed the door.

With a quick check of his breath, a little blow and sniff into the cup of his hand, he followed in her small footsteps.

"What did you tell your mum and dad?" he asked, closing the living room door behind him.

She took the bag from over her shoulder and dropped it to the floor before sitting down on his leather sofa. He leaned back on the door, happy to watch her a moment longer - really take in the sight. She wasn't the first invited here but - most of the time - they never showed up, nor did he find them in the chatroom again to enquire as to why they disappeared.

"I told them I was going to a friend's house," she smiled.

Eleven years old and already quite the seductress; something in those hazel eyes.

Naughty. Rebellious.

The man smiled at her. "Good girl."

She had told her parents, similar in age to the man standing before her, that she was going to a friend's house. They often let her go out by herself - to this particular friend at least - because she only lived around the corner from them. They gave her a time to be home and - to date - she had never let them down.

The man broadened his smile. Yellow, tainted teeth. Stained by nicotine and years of neglect.

"Well," he said, "you're prettier in the flesh."

He wiped the sweat from his forehead and nervously approached. In his mind he was already picturing all that he would do to her; the places he would touch her, the little whimpers she would make as he gave her feelings no one would have yet

had to chance to give her. He sat down next to her, keeping his distance despite

being on top of her in his mind - grinding against her, feeling how tight she is.

How wet she is.

"Thank you," she smiled.

Eleven years old and not a care in the world.

"Can I get you a drink?" he asked.

"Yes, please."

"Wait right there."

He stood up and walked from living room to kitchen, the next door down the

hallway on the right. The kitchen was filthy, a room left to fester whilst he surfed

the chatrooms looking for people to talk to.

Friends to talk to.

Friends to *groom*.

He moved some of the dirty plates from worktop to sink and ran the hot water

to give them a soak. Something in the back of his mind told him that - soon enough

- he'd have what he really wanted and would then be free to tidy up.

Reaching up to the top cupboard, he pulled out the only bottle of squash that

he had.

"Blackcurrant okay?" he called out.

Eleven years old and light-footed.

"Don't you have anything stronger?"

Her voice startled him. An old man's heart quickened in pace. She was standing in the kitchen doorway, casually leaning against the frame. He hadn't even heard her get up from the leather sofa and walk down the corridor. He noticed she'd undone her tie completely. It was hanging there, around the back of her neck, stretching down the front of her shirt. No longer a tie but a tool with which to bind her should she be agreeable to the idea. His mind played out the scenario quick as a flash - her lying on her front with her hands tied behind her back, skirt hitched up, him kissing her buttocks through the cotton of her white panties.

"What did you have in mind?" he asked.

"Got any wine?"

Eleven years old and already knows what she wants from life.

The man raised an eyebrow and looked at her, "Wine?"

She folded her arms and - behind her fringe - raised an eyebrow back, "Is that a problem?"

The man smiled as though scared of making the girl uncomfortable or not giving her what she wanted. He shook his balding head from side to side, "Not at all, here…"

Opening the fridge revealed shelves of leftover food - none of it salad based. Tucked in the side of the door was a half-pint of semi-skinned milk and a bottle of white wine - already opened; not from an evening with company but rather a lonely evening sat in front of a monitor. A few glasses of wine helped him to concentrate and pluck up the courage to talk to the youngsters how he planned. Questions aimed at both sexes. At that age, they were all tight. At that age, he thought, they all had that innocent quality he liked.

He pulled the wine from the fridge and removed the lid before taking two glasses from the draining board. Washing up long since done and left to dry; an owner too lazy to bother putting it away.

"Say when," he told his new friend.

They both watched as the wine reached the top of the glass. He stopped before she said to do so.

"You sure you can handle that?" he asked.

She smiled from the doorway, "I'm a big girl."

Eleven years old. A false confidence already deeply rooted there. She wasn't a big girl. She was petit, almost stick thin. Just the way he liked them.

"Help yourself," he told her as he poured his own glass, also to the top.

The young girl walked into the room and reached for her glass, passing him in the process. Being close to him, he took the opportunity to breathe in her scent. A body spray of sorts, no doubt endorsed by some celebrity singer that girls of that age idolised. He watched as she moved the glass to her lips and took a sip. Full lips so kissable. His mind - deep in the gutter - imaging them wrapped around him.

Her face contorted when the sharp tang of grape engulfed her taste buds. The man tried to hide his smile.

Eleven years old and acting oh so grown up.

"Did you want to go back in the other room?" he asked. "It's more comfortable."

"Sure."

He led the way, wishing it were the other way round and that he was behind, watching her.

Be patient. You'll see all you want soon enough.

The man sat on the edge of the sofa - the same spot he had perched upon earlier when seated next to her. She sat next to him, a little gap between the two, glass still in hand. She took another sip aware that - although she didn't like the taste - she wasn't allowed it at home so she would make the most of it.

He was looking at the bag, a glimmer of hope in his eyes.

"Did you bring it?" he asked.

She followed his gaze to the bag and knew instantly what he was talking about. She set the glass down on the coffee table situated in front of the sofa and reached for her bag. Undoing the leather buckle-strap on the front she flung it open and reached in. He watched intently, the previous glimmer of hope now making his body tingle. He smiled when she withdrew a lilac leotard; her swimming costume.

"That's great," he praised her.

They had communicated online for a few days now and - within hours of talking - he had asked her if she had any pictures of her in a bathing suit. It had been a conversation that came about when she complained that she sometimes felt fat. He told her that he needed to see such a photo so he could get a good idea of what her body looked like without the baggy clothes she was pictured wearing in photos uploaded to her profile.

"I'd love for you to wear it for me sometime," he said, a glint in his eye that gave him away - not as an old man but as a sexual predator. In his mind, he recalled the picture she sent him and how she looked in the costume. More specifically he was picturing the way the tight material of the costume clung to her body - allowing him to imagine her naked - and the way the front clung to her slit leaving little to the imagination. He didn't want her to wear it for him sometime. He wanted her to wear it now and - when she was in it standing before him - he'd compliment her again and then he would ask if he could cuddle her. From there it would move on to suggestions no eleven year old should be witness to. He didn't push her, though. He knew better than that. If she was to wear it, it would be because she believed it to be her choice.

"Maybe," she said.

Eleven-year-old girl slowly coming to her senses.

She looked around the room, temporarily ignoring his leering eyes and the way they slowly undressed her.

"They've gone to stay with my ex-wife," he told her.

"Oh."

He was talking about the imaginary puppies, a lie he had planted early in their online conversation. She had spoken about pets, one of the early questions being whether she had any. She answered that she had a hamster but wanted a dog and that's where his puppies came in. He had a new litter, so young they had yet to open their eyes. Cute little things that fit in the palm of your hand. Of course, she was interested in seeing them when he offered. A conversation that ended with an offer to come round sometime to play with them. Again, it was never forced upon her. It was always her choice. It was her choice to send the picture. It was her choice to meet him a few nights on the trot to continue chatting with him, once she'd finished with her homework, it was her choice to pluck up the courage to lie to her mum and dad to sneak out to see him. Always her choice.

Or so she thought.

"I like your uniform," he said - changing the subject before she asked too many questions that would cause his lie to unravel.

"I hate it."

"Why? You look great in it! Very classy. Although I'll be honest, I do wish you wore your hair in pig-tails like we discussed. That would have made it much smarter," he said. "Can I show you?"

She hesitated a moment, "Sure, I guess."

The man reached forward and took two handfuls of hair from off her shoulder. With a tight grip, he held it away from her slightly to give the impression of having them tied there.

"Very cute," he said, nodding towards a mirror on the far side of the room.

With her hair still gripped by his strong hands, she slowly twisted her head so she could see. Her eyes weren't fixed upon what he was doing to her hair, but the look on his face instead.

An eleven-year-old girl oblivious to the understanding of lust.

In his mind, he was behind her. She was bent over the settee, facing away from him. Her hair - still in his hands. Her screams muffled by the sofa's cushions.

She pulled away from him.

He quickly changed the subject so as to keep the conversation flowing, "Are your friends being nice to you now?" he asked, hiding the lust and replacing it with an insincere smile.

"What do you mean?"

There was a look of panic on her face that he couldn't quite gauge. "You said they were calling you fat and ugly? Remember?"

The conversation had only been a couple of nights ago. It was strange that he would have to remind her of it, especially as she had remembered to pack the costume.

"They're still doing it," she said coyly.

"Kids can be cruel, but I mean what I said; you're not fat." He paused a moment before he started to take it to the next level, "Do you still feel fat?"

"Sometimes."

"That's a pity. I guess it knocks your confidence? You know - if you wanted to - you could be a model."

She laughed, "No I couldn't."

"Of course you could. You're a pretty little thing. You have a nice frame, you have a good height and a nice smile and you have a good head on your shoulders. You're smart, not like other girls of your age. In fact, when I first saw your pictures, I could have sworn an agent would have already picked you up for catalogue work!"

"No they haven't."

"Have you ever sent them any pictures? There's a lot of money involved. Imagine the stuff you could buy. Or holidays for your mum and dad, like when they took you to the beach. You'd like that, wouldn't you? To be able to treat your mum and dad?"

"I guess."

"Here, look…" He jumped up and disappeared from the room. Before she had a chance to do anything, he came back again with a Polaroid camera clutched in his sweaty hands. "Look what I have." He raised the camera, "Here, smile."

Before she could react, he aimed the camera and took a picture. The camera's flash illuminated the room and a couple of seconds later, a photograph slid out of the front. He pulled it away from the camera and waved it in the air a couple of times to speed up the drying process. And then, with a smile, he handed it to the girl.

"See. Pretty little thing."

She looked at the picture and blushed. She looked like a rabbit caught in the headlights.

"You know why your friends call you names?"

She shrugged.

An eleven-year-old girl embarrassed.

"It's because they're jealous."

"Why would they be jealous?"

"Because they know you're pretty and they're plain. I was thinking…" he paused a moment before continuing, "No… No… Forget I said anything."

"What is it?" she asked.

"It's stupid. Forget it."

"Please, tell me."

"Well - okay. I was thinking - would you let me take some more pictures of you? I know some people who work for catalogues and I could probably get you an agent."

"Really?"

An eleven-year-old girl easily led.

"Yes. I mean - if you want to do that." He laughed. "Can you imagine the look on your friends' faces? They'll be so jealous. And no one could call you names then." He took a moment to give her time to think things through. She smiled at the thought of her friends being envious. "What do you say?"

"Okay."

"Okay?"

"Okay!" she exclaimed suddenly confident, suddenly sure of herself.

He beamed again, those stained canines. "Sit up with your back straight," he told her.

She did as he instructed and he started to snap a couple of photos. For each one, he told her something different.

"Smile." Click.

"Look to the left." Click.

"Look to the right." Click.

Each photo spat from the front of the camera, one at a time.

"You're a natural," he said, taking another photo.

He didn't see the pictures as they came out of the camera. He was focused on the pictures that he could have been taking. A young girl with her shirt unbuttoned. A young girl sucking sweetly on a lollipop. A young girl sucking on her index finger whilst staring seductively to the camera. A young girl twiddling with her hair. A young girl with her skirt hitched up, teasing at the panties beneath. A young girl pulling said panties to one side, a reveal of a near-hairless pubic mound.

He lowered the camera, "What about holidays with your mum and dad? Did you like the idea of them?"

"Yes," she said.

Eleven-year-old girl carried away in the moment. The promise of all things shiny and new.

"Catalogues fly their models to nice locations," the man said. "If they think you have what they are looking for - and I know they will love you - this will be easy."

"What do you mean?"

"We take just a couple with you in the swimming costume - maybe get you wet in the shower to make it look as though you've come running out of the sea or something... And we can send them. I know they will go crazy for them and before you know it you'll be flown all over the world with your mum and dad."

"Really?"

"Would I lie to you?"

He had given her wine - not that she drunk it - and he had paid her compliments. But, more importantly than that, he hadn't tried to tell her what she should or shouldn't do and she liked that. It made her feel grown-up.

"Okay."

"You want to do it?"

She nodded.

He tried to contain his excitement - both on his face and between his legs, hidden beneath grey trousers.

"You're going to be a star!" he said. "Why don't you go through to the bathroom and get changed and then, when you're ready, jump in the shower in your costume and give me a shout. Okay?"

"Really?"

"Yes. It's fine. I'll wait here until you're ready for me." He started looking at the pictures he'd already taken, paying her little attention, as though what she were about to do was no big deal to him.

Without another word, she took a hold of the costume - and her bag - and disappeared into the bathroom down the hallway, directed by him calling out when to turn left.

The bathroom door closed and he instantly started picturing her in there, slowly peeling off her clothes until she were standing in the nude. A tight body without a blemish. No ugly sign of ageing. No sagging. No wrinkle. Small breasts starting to form. Few hairs getting in the way of a perfect, untouched vagina. A tight little butt with pert cheeks. One hand on the camera, one hand moving down his body - down his chest to his crotch. A gentle squeeze.

Hard.

He knew his work here was nearly done. She would soon be dressed in the costume he longed to see her in. She'd soon be standing there with water cascading down her. Her skin so perfect and wet. The tightness of the leotard accentuating her figure, pulling into her crack. A shower of water to go with the shower of compliments.

He'd take the photos of her, he'd say how good she is. He'd say they were done and that she could get dressed now. He'd hand her a towel and invite her to take off the costume to dry herself. Slowly peeling the wet fabric away from the skin that it clung so tightly too. But first - before that - he'd give her a big hug at a job well done. By the time he was done, she'd feel so confident and they'd have had so much of a laugh together that it wouldn't seem odd to her. Why would it be? They'd be friends by then. Proper friends - not just because they had met online. Not just chat buddies. They'd be something more because he was helping her do something great with her life. Something that would help her family.

An eleven-year-old girl. Somebody's daughter.

After the hug, he'd hand her the towel and then he would ask her if he could kiss her. The moment of truth. Would he have made such an impression on the young girl that she would say 'yes' - an answer brought about by the fact this man was so cool? Offering her things previously forbidden - photoshoots and alcohol…

Or would she still be this timid little mouse in which case a kiss would not be granted but - instead - taken by force.

Hand still on crotch as he waited for her to call him through, he didn't care which outcome came about now. By the end of the day he would be inside of her and she would be bleeding over him; a hymen ripped from where he'd push through it. On the one hand, it would be nice to hear her say 'yes' and progress things as friends. A thought of him lying upon his back as she painfully eased herself down upon his shaft. But on the other - screams could sometimes be good too.

The bathroom door opened and she stood there - down the hallway - in the lilac costume.

"See - you don't look fat! You look amazing!" he said, sensing she was nervous. "Are you ready?"

She nodded.

He walked towards her - smiling all the way - with the camera by his side. As he got near, he nodded. "Go back into the bathroom." He was pleased to see her follow his instruction with no argument. "Stand by the shower," he said, "and then look back at the camera."

She stood at the shower, he directed her to look as though she were stepping in, and looked back to the camera. She was smiling - albeit a nervous looking smile

- but was soon told to stop. It was better if she didn't smile for this type of shot. At least, that's what he told her.

Click.

The picture printed out and dropped to the floor.

"Bend over slightly, as though you're in mid-move."

She did as she was told and another picture was taken; this picture was put on the side carefully.

"That's good."

"Yeah?" she looked for reassurance.

"Trust me, you're a natural." He lowered the camera. "Okay - get in the shower and turn it on. I want you to look as though you're washing your body with imaginary soap…" In his mind he was already picturing her with a hand between her legs, pressing her inner thigh. Another hand on one of her small breasts. A hopeful wish that the water took a while to warm and made her nipples stand to attention for him just as he was - unseen by her - standing to attention for her.

She stepped into the shower and turned the water on. A slight delay before it cascaded from the shower-head, raining down upon her. He started taking pictures of her when her hands started touching her body - pressing the imaginary bar of soap against herself.

"That is excellent," he said turning his body slightly to hide his true reaction.

An elderly man's wish that it was his hand pressing against her wet skin. His hand, his touch... His tongue...

He took more pictures until there were no more available to take. He set the camera down on the side of the sink and smiled at the girl.

"We're done."

He walked over to the shower and leaned in, soaking his arm in the process, to turn the pouring water off. It slowed and then trickled to a stop. She stood there, shivering from where the water had yet to warm up. Her nipples - as he wished - raised beneath the costume.

"You looked great! My friends at the catalogue will love you. I reckon you'll be working with them in no time."

"Really?" she seemed unsure of herself - no doubt feeling exposed, standing there - shivering - in nothing but a soaking leotard.

"I promise." He patted her on her arm, a move that was supposed to offer reassurance. "I'll get you a towel," he said.

He turned away and she stepped from the shower cubicle, dripping droplets of water onto the tiled floor next to her bag. He pulled the towel from a handrail and turned back to the girl. His eyes went wide and he dropped the towel as the sharp blade pierced his chest with force. He gasped and pulled himself away from the blade.

An eleven-year-old girl standing there, smiling.

Her bag was open. A smile on her face. A kitchen knife in her hand.

The elderly man clutched his chest as blood pumped out and - without a word - he dropped to his knees. He opened his mouth, a want to form a sentence, and blood trickled out. He coughed and some more claret splattered down his chin and onto the floor, mixing with the puddles of water from having the shower on without closing the cubicle door.

"I know what you are," the girl told him. There was no fear in her eyes. There was no emotion in her monotone voice. She was completely calm. She bent over and put the knife back in the school bag, from where she'd taken it when he turned his back. She stepped forward and snatched the towel from his hand and - with both bag and towel in hand - she walked from the room.

The man tried to get up but instead fell forward, stopping himself from face planting with a hand to the floor - keeping one pressed to his chest. He could feel himself getting colder as the blood seeped from between his fingers and continued leaking from his mouth - choking him in the process. He tried again to call out but nothing came, merely a splutter. He rolled onto his side as a numbness started to spread through his limbs.

In the living room the girl peeled away her wet costume. Letting it drop to the floor, she stepped out of it - naked and wet. A smile on her face as she imagined him bleeding out in the next room, picturing the look on his face if only he could see her now. She patted herself dry with the towel and started to put her school uniform on once more, fishing it from the bag she'd stored it in to keep it dry and free from splatter.

Less than five minutes and she was dressed and out of the door with the same bag over her shoulder - containing nothing but a wet costume, a damp towel and a bloodied blade. Whistling a tune, she skipped merrily down the stairs towards the apartment complex's entrance. Out of the door and across the road - she continued - to where a car was parked.

Eleven-year-old girl being picked up by a loving mum and dad.

"How did it go, sweetie?" her father asked, looking at her via the rear-view mirror.

"It's done," she said sweetly, putting the bag down in the foot well before sitting back and fastening her seat-belt.

"We're proud of you, honey," her father continued. "And your sister would be too."

Her mother didn't say anything. She was sitting in the front of the car clutching a photograph; a family at a beach - a mother, a father, a girl in a lilac swimming costume and a second, slightly older girl. A tear rolled from the mother's cheek and splashed the photograph. It didn't go unnoticed by the father of the girl. He leaned over and gave his wife's leg a squeeze. She looked up at him and he smiled.

"It's done," he said. "Your daughter did well."

His wife - the girl's mother - smiled back at him. She turned to her daughter in the back of the car.

"Thank you," she said.

"When can we do it again?" the girl asked as she casually flicked through the photographs the old man snapped of her. She had collected them from around his apartment, making sure as to leave none of them behind. Not just because they were evidence but mainly because she thought she looked good in them.

For a dirty old pervert, he sure did manage to capture her good side.

Eleven-year-old girl. Someone's daughter. Someone's sister. No one's victim.

End.

Love Matt Shaw? Seen his Fan Club?

Early access to books, free short stories, signed books posted direct to your door and MORE!

https://www.patreon.com/TheMattShaw?ty=h

www.mattshawpublications.co.uk

www.facebook.com/mattshawpublications

With thanks to

Joan MacLeod, Alicia Green, Barry Skelhorn, Kelly Rickard, Leah Cruz, Hayley Marcham, Nancy Loudin, Nicola Kidd, Michelle Clevenger, Suzanne Elliott, Cece Romano, Andy Astle, Jennifer Eversole, Debbie Dale, Andrea Stevenson, Paul James, Kim Tomsett, Angela McBride, Chad Ferguson, Grant Oxford, Scott Hunter, Sophie Hall, Jennifer Pelfrey, Stacy Latini, Jarod Barbee, Colleen Cassidy, Frank Meyers, Gilly Adam.

Your continued support means the world to me.

Thank you.

Made in the USA
Middletown, DE
08 December 2017